THE MAGIC DOGS OF SAN VICENTE

ESSENTIAL PROSE SERIES 129

THE MAGIC DOGS OF SAN VICENTE

MARK FISHMAN

GUERNICA
EDITIONS
TORONTO · BUFFALO · LANCASTER (U.K.)
2016

Michael Mirolla, editor
Cover design and interior layout, David Moratto
Guernica Editions Inc.
1569 Heritage Way, Oakville, (ON), Canada L6M 2Z7
2250 Military Road, Tonawanda, N.Y. 14150-6000 U.S.A.
www.guernicaeditions.com

Distributors:
University of Toronto Press Distribution,
5201 Dufferin Street, Toronto (ON), Canada M3H 5T8
Gazelle Book Services, White Cross Mills, High Town,
Lancaster LA1 4XS U.K.

First edition.

Legal Deposit — First Quarter
Library of Congress Catalog Card Number: 2015949356
Library and Archives Canada Cataloguing in Publication Fishman,
Mark, 1954-, author
The magic dogs of San Vicente / Mark Fishman. — First edition.

(Essential prose series ; 129)
Issued also in print and electronic formats.
ISBN 978-1-77183-078-2 (paperback).--ISBN 978-1-77183-079-9
(epub).--ISBN 978-1-77183-080-5 (mobi)

I. Title. II. Series: Essential prose series ; 129

PS3606.I835M34 2016   813'.6   C2015-905880-5   C2015-905881-3

Not just purgatory but hell awaits
those who could have done good and did not do it.
It is the reverse
of the beatitude that the Bible has
for those who are saved,
for the saints,
who could have done wrong and did not.
Of those who are condemned it will be said:
They could have done good and did not.

—Oscar Romero, July 16, 1977

Crouched down behind some big rocks, a little dirt from the earth blown in circles by the wind, and another gust throwing small dry twigs and pebbles up in the air, the Flores brothers, still breathing heavily, they'd been running without looking behind them, using their legs for all they were worth, José Matías and Wilber Eduardo, not far from San Esteban Catarina, a stone's throw if you had a good arm, rallying the courage to lift their heads up from behind the boulder to look at a dapple-gray horse neighing, raising its head, lowering it, nodding like it was agreeing to something, the Flores brothers asking it with their eyes what'd happened to them, the horse returning their looks without saying anything, just nodding, it was a magnificent animal, a horse in all its majesty, not some mangy sway-backed creature out of a nightmare, and they thought that maybe, after all, it wasn't agreeing to anything, it hadn't been there a minute ago when they'd made for the rocks, so where'd it come from, the Flores brothers like crazy people straight out of the nuthouse, but the dapple-gray was there, standing on the other side of the rock, a really big stone, maybe part of a megalithic monument, or something a glacier had left in its tracks, nothing exceptional, really big almost round boulders, no monument, but a lucky break, they'd found them not long after they took off running, a few minutes later, after they'd seen something they figured they'd never see again, finding a few large rocks gathered together, a sort of deposit of enormous stones, big enough to hide behind, and the Flores brothers, ready to throw in the towel right now and die where they were, crouched safely behind a boulder with a dapple-gray horse watching them under an early sun in the blazing heat of morning.

José Matías and Wilber Eduardo, Graciela Menéndez, Gustavo and Emiliano, Lucía and Concepción, Benavides and Alfonso, and little Margó, it was her birthday, Margó drinking from a bottle of orange soda, it was hot and she was thirsty, José Matías and Wilber Eduardo, Emiliano and Lucía, Concepción and Gustavo and Benavides, Alfonso and Margó, no one saying a word, an angel passing overhead, a break with lots of suspense, then Graciela, what do you think you'll get for your birthday, Margó? the Flores brothers, between sips and swallows, and Wilber Eduardo, a short recitation, *Zan nican temoc y xochimiquiztli tlalpan, / aci yehua ye nican,* "Here on earth the flowery death has descended, / it is coming near," a couple of lines from a poem, José Matías, narrowing his eyes, that's what we thought was happening to us, we all remember, don't we, like it was yesterday, and Graciela Menéndez and the others, they all heard the words pitched at them, struck in the face both in Náhuatl and in translation, not questioning for an instant what they'd understood of the Uto-Aztecan language, relating directly to their own experiences, joined harmoniously with the two lines of poetry by Axayacatl, the son of a Mexica prince and a lady from Tlacopan, words confirming what they were thinking now, on account of what José Matías and Wilber Eduardo had just said, and what they'd been through, arrest and torture and round-the-clock fear that couldn't possibly be the result of not sleeping with their feet pointing south to avoid the evil eye, "a man is no more free of his past than his body," and Concepción, now's not the time, *mis amigos,* it's Margó's birthday, and the rest of them agreeing, let's forget about it, and Gustavo, you're right, Concha, it isn't the time or the place, our story isn't meant for the ears of a child, what a fucked up world, all of them except Margó sighing a big choral sigh.

They were sitting outside under a hot sun — all the windows in the house were open and it was still so hot you could fry an egg on the tiled floor — neighbors and friends, a birthday celebration, each a welcome guest of the other, and everyone sitting as still as they could sit in the roasting afternoon, without a water hose to cool them off, Concepción smoking a cigarillo, a beer in Gustavo's hand, Graciela Menéndez rubbing lotion on her arms, Margó, putting the bottle of orange soda down, clapping her hands, it was her birthday party, she'd come with Alfonso, an uncle like a second father to her, on account of Margó's parents who were killed in San Salvador, not so long ago, an incompetent, messed up shoot-out between *maras* — *la vida entre las maras* — and the *Sombra negra,* another tragedy, in a long line of tragedies, with plenty of weeping, if it isn't that it's this, or is it the other way around, and Alfonso, Graciela's neighbor, always with a book in his hand, Benavides whistling at the branches of a tree, a bird maybe, and Lucía and Emiliano, Emiliano eating a *pupusa revuelta* of pork, beans, cheese, with loroco, called *quilite,* and a big spoonful of *curtido,* fermented cabbage relish, and a very spicy tomato salsa on the side, despite the fact that he couldn't digest pork and chiles like he used to, they all agreed that you retain only what you think is significant, life is like that, not like retaining water, your body filling up, fattening up, it may be uncomfortable but it isn't noteworthy, and Graciela Menéndez, so, *mis amigos,* our Flores brothers, let's not talk about the past, we've been through enough, Margó's been through enough, so scarred and urgently in need of repair, and Wilber Eduardo, it was just a little something by Axayacatl, Water-Face, an Aztec Emperor, shrugging his shoulders, José Matías putting his hand on his brother's neck, gently squeezing it, reassuring him, voice definitely audible, it's ok, *mi hermano,* leave the poetry for later.

Emiliano, with his mouth full, swallowing without chewing, knowing it'll destroy his belly, talking about whatever came to his mind, kites heading north fly hundreds of feet above the earth, ducks never touch the ground, they just fly by, waving farewell, but nobody listening, Emiliano, a forceful voice with peppery breath, my guts are burning, *hermana,* speaking to no one, speaking to everyone, maybe a suicide attempt with a *pupusa revuelta* in my hand, you've got to hand it to me — and Concepción, interrupting him, hang on, El Puño, she always called him the Fist, don't be so self-centered, thinking of yourself, inconsideration not indigestion is what you ought to worry about, keep your mind on why we're here, not what's in your hand, you knew those chiles would knock you out, TKO, and Emiliano, okay Concha okay, and Concepción, a cloud of smoke from a cigarillo, it's Margó's birthday, let's sing another birthday song, looking at the others, and the others, laughter rising, tumbling to the ground, Graciela clapping her hands to a rhythm in her head, Emiliano, how about another mouthful instead, chewing slowly this time, smiling, nodding at Concepción, looking at Lucía for support, just kidding around, *pequeña,* winking at Margó, Margó winking back, and Emiliano, a column of confidence not a pillar of smoke on account of he'd swallowed a handful of Trumpet Brand Seirogan gastrointestinal pills from Osaka this morning after breakfast, Emiliano, I won't deny myself some pleasure, not now, not ever, even if it kills me, and everyone laughing but Lucía, who couldn't remember if they had more industrial-strength indigestion tablets waiting at home.

José Matías and Wilber Eduardo, crouching down behind some really big rocks, like there weren't any strong and leafy *tempisque* trees to climb in order to stay out of the hands of trouble, but there were *tempisque,* and plenty of other trees, too, the *tihuilote* trees, maybe the big balsam tree — *bálsamo del Perú* — and its vanilla-scented resin, but no, they were far away from the western Pacific coast, so maybe a White Sapote, known as *cochitzapotl,* trees for them to hide behind standing just another two hundred yards away, which gave plenty of shade for anyone who bothered to run an extra two hundred yards, but not the Flores brothers, they were out of breath, and José Matías, who smoked Delta Reds, so forget about him making another two hundred yards without dropping dead, and the barbed wire and stone fence, you could've hidden behind the stone fence, crawled on your hands and knees, the *cadejos* would've protected you from there on, the magic dogs appearing where they least expected it, maybe from San Esteban Catarina, or San Vicente, it was a secret, it was nothing, only the Flores brothers stopped at the big round boulders, short of breath, not knowing the *cadejos* were anywhere near them, they'd have to find José Matías and Wilber Eduardo, the *cadejos* up to the task, with weather eyes open, always, just sniffing them out, here's one, there's the other, and maybe Wilber Eduardo, breathing hard through his mouth, maybe he could've gone on, but he drew in the reins of endurance out of sympathy for his brother, who smoked like a chimney.

The magic dogs weren't far away — unusual in daylight — they were resting beneath a rare Mexican yew, not thinking the Flores brothers were in trouble, at least nothing urgent, and so hot in the sun and dry wind that a siesta was the right thing, now for a few minutes, to close their eyes, two magic dogs that didn't pay attention to the seasons, they didn't know which season it was, this one or that one, the temperature was their guide, it didn't seem to matter if it was day or night, a siesta, and the *cadejos* — instead of paws, they had hooves like a deer — a yawn, the *cadejos* were stretched out on the ground beneath an evergreen shrub, the Mexican yew, a landscape imagined or real, while the horse without a rider nodded its head at José Matías and Wilber Eduardo.

The Flores brothers and the silence of the sky above them, silence filled with unheard voices, then a bird gave a long high-pitched shriek to break the stillness, waking them from a frightened sleep with their eyes open, José Matías and Wilber Eduardo, trembling and sweating extravagantly beneath the broiling sun, drawn back behind not-so-perfectly-round boulders with broad shoulders worn smooth by erosion, shrugging beneath an over-flying White-breasted Hawk, its dark upperparts almost black, thighs whitish-buff and under parts and cheeks entirely white.

The screeching hawk shot through the sky above them, as fast as it had appeared it was gone, and the Flores brothers squinted up to find it but saw nothing — wearing sunglasses but squinting just the same — so they got to thinking about the past, a thousand years ago, it was that far away, and they couldn't help but remember even if they didn't want to think about it, the bird's shriek was like a man's cry, it was a cry they'd heard before that had everything to do with men like General Juan Humberto Reyes Vehemente, and General José Enrique Embustera, to give a name to a couple of faces, maybe it was both of them, or it wasn't them at all, it didn't much matter to the Flores brothers, there were sergeants, captains, majors, lieutenant-colonels, a range of soldiers inflicting punishments on those who hadn't done anything, who lived and believed correctly — and one of them had been there, maybe just Reyes Vehemente, at that moment Director-General of the Salvadoran National Guard, but who can say, and José Matías and Wilber Eduardo, a private interrogation, they were blindfolded and didn't see his face, they might've recognized General Reyes Vehemente's voice, his polished boots, or maybe both generals were there, and if they were, then one had his hands clasped behind his back, and the other, José Enrique Embustera, his arms were straight down at his sides, but if they weren't there, at least the orders had come from them, from Reyes Vehemente or José Enrique Embustera, shooting down from above like malevolent stars, and the orders were carried out to the letter, as it's always said, by imbeciles, by soldiers who were fanatically willing to dish out pain, soldiers dirtying their hands with blood and piss and shit as if there was something powerful attracting them; if General Reyes Vehemente was standing nearby, out of sight but within range of hearing the goings-on, he glanced furtively at his pocket watch, waiting impatiently to eat his lunch.

The Flores brothers, José Matías and Wilber Eduardo, captured and beaten, flown in a helicopter, on their way to El Paraíso, a garrison, before reaching the National Guard headquarters, together in a cell a hundred yards away from the room with a concrete floor and a long table and a metal bed-frame, a sort of *parrilla,* and a bucket of water as big as a tub, the room where interrogations were held, José Matías and Wilber Eduardo, tortured, hearing the national anthem everyday at 6:00 a.m., they were witnesses, at first hand, to the burned corpse wrapped in a plastic sheet thrown out onto the cement floor in front of them, stinking like burned roast pork, nauseating and sweet, stop staring and pick it up you sons of a bitch, what are you looking at? don't drop it, *¡pendejos!* follow the sergeant out with it, *¡frágil!* the lieutenant shouted, laughing, it was so funny, and now, hiding behind some big rocks, boulders, José Matías and Wilber

Eduardo spoke the words without saying them: "They took out their knives and stuck them under his fingernails; after they took his fingernails off, then they broke his elbows; afterwards they gouged out his eyes; then they took their bayonets and sliced his skin all around his chest, arms, and legs; they then took his hair off and the skin of his scalp, and when they saw there was nothing left to do with him, they threw gasoline on him and burned him."

José Matías and Wilber Eduardo, opening their eyes hidden on the back side of two pairs of sunglasses, large metal Ray-Ban Aviators, Wilber Eduardo smiling an uncomfortable smile, sunglasses reflecting the bright sunlight, the two brothers facing each other, blinking, crouched down behind some big rocks, a neighing horse nearby, José Matías and Wilber Eduardo saying in the same voice at the same time that it was a sin, a real sin, not one of those things you say when you mean that it's a shame, but a real sin that goes straight up to heaven, written in a book up there for everyone to read who gets there, and they couldn't forget a horror they'd seen and smelled, that stinking body burnt to a crisp, the smell, and that once-was-a-living-human-being that would stay with them for the rest of their lives with no chance of fragrant *resedo* flowers falling like tears from the sky.

They weren't often easily frightened since the day they had to carry a body wrapped in a plastic sheet out to where they dumped bodies that nobody'd see ever again, it'd been enough for anybody to their dying day; now they were trembling on account of what they'd seen, overwhelmed by an anxiousness that weighed a ton, the oxygen held back in their lungs, and what they knew and what they didn't know about what they'd seen today was piled one layer on top of the other and stood as high as a skyscraper leaning into the bright sun; it wasn't the same kind of fear, nothing like the torture and the body they carried away, but, still, it was more than they could bear.

So, José Matías and Wilber Eduardo, talking without speaking, a kind of telepathy saying, the clock's ticking, let's think of everything we can and do nothing about it, no — so the clock's ticking, and do we get up from behind these stones and get back up on the horse we fell off of? in a manner of speaking, and climb into the pickup truck and drive off to find a solution, straighten it out, once and for all, or do we stay here, shivering even though it isn't cold, like we're going to have a heart attack from fright, seeking answers to questions without answers, you and me, after all we've been through, brother, dropping dead, at the same time right here.

Like it could hear what they were thinking by means other than the known senses, the dapple-gray horse turned its back on them after fluttering its eyelashes, a flirting girl, the horse turned on its hooves and started to walk away, not slightly in a hurry, a slow gait — no trot, gallop, pace or canter — away from the Flores brothers hiding behind a few boulders, proof in capital letters that it knew exactly what they were thinking.

And what they were thinking now amounted to a plan of little genius but great necessity because José Matías had left his cigarettes in the glove compartment of the pickup and it was time for a smoke, you mean you really got to have a cigarette, now? and Wilber Eduardo, shaking his head, no way, brother, but knowing it was going to be that way if José Matías said so, and like that it was one two three and up off their knees and standing in the bright sunlight for all the world to see like they were being pursued in a Western, the pistols were loaded and they were going to shoot it out while making a break for it.

The *cadejos* were standing by, nothing and nobody told them to get up from lying beneath a Mexican yew to make the two hundreds yards in seconds flat, the blink of an eye, really, but that was how the *cadejos* worked when they were on the job, standing on their hooves just behind José Matías and Wilber Eduardo, who were signed up in two opposing parties, brothers divided by the desire of one over the reason of the other, one a minority of cautious timidity in disagreement with his brother, the other, an outspoken proponent of his own needs who proceeded to intone with a purposeful whisper that they'd better be going on their way, horse or no horse, to the pickup truck.

The Flores brothers fanned away the sweat that poured from their pores out of fear and the heat of the merciless sun, and the *cadejos* accompanied them around the boulders, dirt from the earth blown by the wind in circles and throwing small dry twigs in their faces, the four of them, dogs and man, Wilber Eduardo, and the guardian angel must watch over us, Wilber Eduardo crossing himself, believing in guardian angels, not seeing or hearing the *cadejos* walking soundlessly beside them on their deerlike hooves in a landscape straight out of the Bible, when was the last time you were in a church, and his brother meant it but said it sarcastically, I need a smoke, and you're my brother.

The first sign straight out of the Bible, the first promise, the welcoming abundance of nature — the mystery of the world was a world of mystery, where forests once stood, now cleared and farmed land — a twenty-five-foot-tall *jocote* tree with its edible ripening red oval drupe, or stone fruit, eaten ripe with or without the skin — sometimes eaten unripe with salt and vinegar or lime juice — and José Matías and Wilber Eduardo walked around it, looking up at the fruit, while following in the walking gait of the horse, who kept on nodding its head as if to say they were heading in the right direction, don't turn back, my brothers, have courage and you'll be safe when you get to your truck and turn the key in the ignition to start it up, and don't forget the pleasure of that first hit off the cigarette; and the second sign was a *cica,* a plant like a palm with hard palm leaves but not at all a palm tree, spreading its spiky long fingers out into the sunlight, with narrow, thick leaflets, it was often confused with a palm but it's a cycad, and it reached out at the Flores brothers with paired, horny razor-sharp spines.

Wilber Eduardo turned his head to look back at the *jocote* tree, thought of the syrup made of panela, *jocote* and mango, and licked his lips, tasted the sweetness on his tongue, and when he looked at where he was going, straight ahead at the grasslands rolling out in front of him on the central high plateau in the eastern interior that lay between two mountain ranges, and maybe at the volcano San Vicente — Vince is a prince, José Matías said, without missing a beat — known as Chinchontepec, *Las Chiches,* the Jiboa Valley stretching out northeast and north of the western summit, Wilber Eduardo immediately lowered his gaze, rolled his eyes, and realized the horse wasn't there, they weren't following anything but their own path toward the pickup, so he nudged his brother with his elbow, José Matías, marching for his cigarettes, chin up, Wilber Eduardo thrusting his own chin forward in the direction of the nothing-like-a-horse landscape, giving José Matías a frown from behind his sunglasses, his brother raised his Ray-Bans, shook his head, Wilber Eduardo smiled a smile of defeat, together they shook their heads, and they were wondering whether they'd imagined the horse in this land of enchanted and treacherous volcanoes that gave the earth its fertility and influenced the mood of stars and terrestrial bodies and humankind.

At that point, far away from their past, with *Las Chiches* watching them, proud or not they couldn't tell from where they were walking with the volcano in the distance, quite a distance, the Flores brothers realized something serious was happening, and the ascending emotion of their immersion in a new kind of fear dropped on their heads with the weight of the three boulders they'd been hiding behind after what they'd seen sent them on the run, leaving a pickup truck, and what was in it, to stand in the broiling sun. Offsetting the worrying effect of a horse that either was or was not there a minute ago, José Matías and Wilber Eduardo, finding fault with themselves for having seen or not seen but definitely thinking and believing they saw a horse leading them away from the *jocote* tree and some big rocks, boulders to hide behind, boulders to help them forget or ignore the frightening thing they saw in the bright light of day — offsetting it all was José Matías' concentration while champing at the cigarette bit that wasn't yet in his teeth, and a thirst for something sweet on Wilber Eduardo's part, after having tasted the syrup made of panela, *jocote* and mango, imaginary but saliva-inducing, the two of them knowing there was something like salvation waiting for them in the pickup.

José Matías and Wilber Eduardo, surveying the landscape, a look to the left, a look to the right, kicking up a little dirt with their Western-style boots, no horse, no hawk, no threat from the apparition they'd seen that made them take off like a couple of forest rabbits, tapetis, under the hot sun, and they thought they'd left the doors of the truck open wide on the wild landscape but they were shut and locked, so José Matías reached in his trousers pocket for the keys, Wilber Eduardo let his hand drop for a second onto the hood which burned him slightly before he snapped it away from the flame.

They settled themselves in the cab with an abundance of heat and a case of twelve-ounce cans of Kolashampan Bravo under a tarp in the bed of the truck behind them, half a dozen vacuum-sealed plastic bags of one hundred percent natural San Andrés brand *Jocote rojo* and several glass jars of Miguel's Changungas, or nance fruit, in syrup on the floor in the front beneath the dash, a couple of packs of

Delta Reds, not *mentolados,* on the seat, an open pack in the glove compartment, and almost smoking by themselves in the heat with the windows rolled up.

José Matías went for the glove compartment like a dope fiend, Wilber Eduardo didn't pay his brother any attention, but sighed, craving something pleasantly clean, pure, and cool to drink, José Matías lit up, switched on the ignition and the air from the air conditioner shot out of the vents with a vengeance and behind the initial gust of counterfeit wind came the rancid smell of the burst guts of a public-domain mongrel, filling their nostrils, a gasp from the pair of them, they both started to choke, the Flores brothers feeling sick, despite the cigarette that hung from José Matías' lips, burning cheap tobacco that could've hidden any smell but the smell of a dead dog.

So how did a dead mongrel decked out in moth-eaten fur land under the hood and downwind of the air conditioner where we'd smell it and choke to death, José Matías and Wilber Eduardo, jumping out of the cab into the burning hot sun, pinching their noses shut, covering their mouths with a free hand and gagging from the smell; José Matías threw his cigarette away as soon as his feet hit the ground, Wilber Eduardo stomped his white shoes, shaking his long black hair slicked back on his head with Vaseline and Brylcreem.

They raised the hood of the truck and looked in at the corpse, wishing they'd found a pomegranate tree there instead, then checked their pockets by patting them down with the palms of their hands — maybe they'd carried gloves in them — but didn't find anything, go get a newspaper out of the cab, José Matías, I'll keep an eye on it so it doesn't disappear, by sleight of hand, like it got there, and Wilber Eduardo, his brother, after saying what he'd said, nothing more, kept on shaking his head until his hair fell down in front of his face.

The newspaper didn't really help them even though they'd read it, the animal's fur was stuck to the hot parts of the engine and the underside of the hood that'd been sitting in the blistering heat of the sun for more than an hour, but they used the paper sheets to protect their hands and pried the thing off what it was stuck to, top and bottom, each turning his head away, tucking his chin into his chest to keep out the direct get-the-drift of the rotten smell of burst guts; they dropped it, and the mongrel made a thump when it hit the ground; a whispered hissing sound, the air expelled or the gas escaped.

There wasn't a mountain pine or oak tree near the cleared land where they'd left the pickup, not far from San Esteban Catarina, a municipality in the department of San Vicente — a parish priest, Alirio Napoleón Macías, was killed there by a paramilitary group on August 4, 1979 — cleared land where there wasn't a dead branch from a dead tree to scrape off the parts of the mongrel stuck to the engine and underside of the hood, instead, an old wool plaid shirt behind the seat in the cab, torn into rectangles and used to wipe clean the foul surfaces.

José Matías, a grim expression on his face, the *Sihuanaba* must've put it there, and Wilber Eduardo confirming his brother's words with a nod of his head, and the *cadejos* right there but unseen, wearing clothes of daylight and air, invisible and standing guard over the Flores brothers, Wilber Eduardo crossing himself again, the guardian angels aren't protecting us, that's pretty obvious, and José Matías giving his brother a frown, a few words that were like a frown, spirits that're supposed to watch over and protect us are around here somewhere, his reassuring voice, and just the same, José Matías, disappointed and not convinced that a mongrel cooking on the engine of the truck — the unmistakable work of a *Sihuanaba* — fell into the sphere of responsibility for a guardian angel, maybe for the *cadejos,* it was more than likely, but could they appear in daylight and where were they? José Matías was convinced of nothing but the craving he had for another cigarette, the first lost to the stink of the moment and the need to get out of the truck, so he lit another one, drew in a lungful and exhaled, truly satisfied with the taste of the Delta Reds.

Wilber Eduardo, trying to remember if they'd seen a shape-changing spirit in the form of a beautiful, long-haired woman, maybe washing clothes, a *Sihuanaba,* who lured men away from their planned routes only to lose them in deep canyons before revealing her horse's face, and José Matías, leaning against the cab, worrying, the terrible fear of everything after what'd happened to them, and the sorrows of having been born at all, worrying like only the Flores brothers worry, José Matías, a creased forehead, maybe consternation, smoking his cigarette.

They'd seen a dapple-gray horse, Wilber Eduardo knew this because his heart told him so, and he was sure ever after, and then José Matías confirmed it when his brother asked him, exhaling another cloud, but the horse they saw was a solid-hoofed plant-eating domesticated mammal with a flowing mane and tail, a real horse on four legs with hooves planted firmly on terrestrial ground — without profuse weeping, a sign of worry, no weeping at all, and to be sure to protect themselves from the *Sihuanaba,* whether they'd seen it or not, the Flores brothers, before getting into the pickup, the pickup's engine running like a charm, the two brothers took turns biting the machete — not too hard, not too soft, and no chewing — that they kept under the seat in the cab.

José Matías and Wilber Eduardo, counting seconds that passed as they got further away from the mongrel's corpse rotting in the merciless heat of the sun, and there was the *Sihuanaba* to keep in mind, whether she was following them or not — contrary to the legend which would have them following her — but the Flores brothers, José Matías smoking his third cigarette, and Wilber Eduardo drinking the syrup from an open glass jar of Miguel's Changungas — he'd devoured the nance fruit faster than they'd left behind the dead dog with José Matías' foot pressed down hard on the accelerator — the Flores brothers rode in the pickup headed southeast in the direction of Río Lempa, José Matías and Wilber Eduardo wanting to lose themselves and find themselves, they wanted everything at once, sitting comfortably in the pickup ranging the seismic bumps and curves in the road taking them away from the apparition that had frightened them.

The sun burns away our weakness, José Matías — you felt it like I felt it pouring down hot as lava from *Las Chiches* — and in our case, speaking for the two of us, impotence, fear, stress, and worrying, too, they're our weaknesses, so I want the word to go out — are you listening? — okay, we're cautious, it's all right, this isn't torture, not like what we went through, not shot in the left forearm, no alligator clips and electric shocks, we aren't hung up by our hands — they called it the plane, like we'd ever forget! — what we're afraid of won't kill us, not today, so there's nothing to worry about, maybe the heat of the sun burned our weakness away, but I don't believe it, otherwise — really, this is too much for me — scared is for kids, so we aren't kids, definitely, on account of our age, sixty, sixty-two — I'm making a speech, you don't have to tell me, there are times I talk a lot, too much, maybe I'm nervous, but what I'm saying, what I'm trying to say is, well, what *is* this? and José Matías, we're running away, the only words that came out of his mouth, José Matías, downshifting, flipping his cigarette, the butt, through the crack of the open window, watching it tumble weightlessly in the air, eyes back on the road, seismic bumps jolting the cab, buckled up and safely in their pickup, the Flores brothers heading toward Río Lempa and far from what scared them.

Wilber Eduardo, waiting for more from José Matías, but not another word, his brother shifting into high gear, a grunt, that's all he heard, Wilber Eduardo, high priest of *yuca frita,* wiping nance-fruit syrup from his lips with a handkerchief, looking at his watch, an imitation, the original costs a fortune, a birthday present from Gustavo, I can't afford a real one, it's the best imitation money can buy, you'll have to take my word for it, and Wilber Eduardo, his birthday and

a big smile, you're a real friend, I won't take it off, never —
unless I'm washing dishes in a sink full of water; and now,
Wilber Eduardo, looking at his watch, and the time, one-
forty, Wilber Eduardo, he looked at José Matías, saying, an
additional fact to keep in mind, *mi hermano* — are you listening? — the sun like the *flor de isote* will beg our pardon,
conclusively, for keeping our impotence, fear and stress for
as long as we have to while we're alive, so you and me, tri-
umphant and wrapped in waves of applause, we're going to
find the exceptional detail which explains it, the apparition
— in daylight! — so distant, and at the same time so close
and distinct I can still see it.

The *cadejos* didn't leave them, the Flores brothers didn't
know if they'd left them or not because they hadn't seen them
in the first place, but the *cadejos* were riding dreamily in
the back next to the case of twelve-ounce cans of Kolashampan Bravo lying under a tarp, and the wind ripped through
the back of the pickup, whipping the tarp which flapped like
a big black wing, the magic dogs weren't disturbed by the
wind and the sound of the wind, and felt nothing but the
sensation of flying through limitless time untold by man
with their sleepy dog's eyes closed, the bumpy ride didn't
bother them either, they just stretched out their legs, rested
their chins on them, and tucked their noses under the edge
of the tarp where it was tied down, out of the flow of wind.

The river showed its shining face to the sky, with the
sunlight stretching out across its surface sending stars into

the air that hung there for an instant just above it, and the Flores brothers, with the engine running, strained their ears for the sound of the splash of fish and the flapping wings of birds in flight, José Matías, lighting a cigarette, blowing the smoke out the open window as the pickup idled at the roadside, no birds, no fish, exhaust fumes washing into the cab through the open window, the limpid Lempa, river of their dreams, they really saw it or they imagined they were looking at it while parked at the side of the road, maybe a bridge spanning the river, but it was Río Acahuapa, they were heading toward Chamoco, look over there, José Matías and Wilber Eduardo, without knowing it they were waiting for the *cadejos* to finish drinking a little of the river's fresh water, waiting without seeing them — the *cadejos'* eyes shone at night like hot coals, and they didn't like it when someone looked back at them when they were following a person to protect them — the *cadejos,* thirsty under the sun, thirsty for no movement at all, the pickup sprinting through the dry air — ruffled fur against the wind — it's a real savage, that river, or I mean, it's the wind that's savage from the bed of a pickup on *la Carretera Panamericana,* the Central American Highway 1, and the Flores brothers gave it a last look, San Vicente not far behind them, Chinchontepec, *Las Chiches,* with the river Lempa ahead, they couldn't see it from there, and Usulután department beyond, and the *cadejos,* sticking their noses under the edge of the tarp, raising it, climbed back into the bed of the truck.

Wilber Eduardo, I'm feeling the strange emotion of not knowing what life is anymore, *mi hermano,* and it comes from what we saw rising out of nowhere in front of us like some ghost or monster in a Mexican horror movie, maybe *El grito de la muerte,* or *El hombre y el monstruo,* it throws me off, and no matter what you think, I can tell by the way you're concentrating on the road that it doesn't put you on cloud nine either, no jumping for joy with life, not you or me — we've been through enough already, those fucking generals, fucking everybody serving the government, things are bad for people born here, and those generals, Reyes Vehemente and José Enrique Embustera, may they rot in hell when they get there, *mi hermano,* because they'll send them back here, a judgement on their lives — at least one of them, what do you want to bet? and that's better than nothing, deported like the worms they are, that's what ought to happen, and the Department of Homeland Security, *en el Norte* — like it or not, and I don't like it — they started the ball rolling, Reyes Vehemente and José Enrique Embustera, they lost the case in court, at least one of them will get sent back here — maybe then the *cuilios* we've got now will fuck them up good, give them a little of their own medicine — but I won't hold my breath, we know better than that, can you imagine? sent back here, that's a laugh, but eight months ago, an immigration judge saying Reyes Vehemente can be deported on account of the rights charges against him — am I dreaming? — pinch me, *mi hermano,* from West Palm Beach to here, I read somewhere he lives in Palm Coast, Florida, the motherfucker, and Reyes Vehemente, he already paid out three hundred large, that's three-hundred thousand six years ago, they lost the case in 2002, it was to the tune of fifty-four point six million, total — just try and count it on your fingers, *mi hermano* — I hope they shit their pants, both of them, who shit on honorable people like us, and I've really got to wash my hands, they're sticky with *changungas* syrup.

José Matías, not looking at his brother, nodding his head, okay, you're right, I feel like I've seen a ghost, maybe a monster out of a Mexican movie, I'm a bit sick in my stomach on account of it, okay? there's something you can wipe your hands on in the glove compartment, and while you're in there, get me another pack of cigarettes, will you? José Matías, keeping his eyes on *la Carretera Panamericana,* looking for a turnoff, maybe an off-ramp, but more likely a junction or an intersection, it wasn't a big highway right there, just before they entered a small town, maybe a village, and slowing down enough to read the signs along the road, or no signs at all, because José Matías knew where he was going, turning off just before the Lempa on a secondary highway running north, and in due course they'd pass little San Lorenzo to the east, not the San Lorenzo north of Atiquizaya, the Flores brothers, they were heading toward the town of Lajas y Canoas.

A document in the Flores brothers' hands, not very long ago, it felt like yesterday, Wilber Eduardo, a printout, you can get your hands on anything these days, and José Matías, not volcanoes and a cure for old age, *mi hermano,* but thanks to our cousin, Luz, who's as talented as a magician with these machines, and Wilber Eduardo, fumbling with the first page, confirming what his brother was saying, computers, you're right, it's here in our hands faster than the mail and without a postman, one brother looking over the other's shoulder, these pages, hang on, don't turn them so fast, the pages sending words of contentment to weary eyes that open and shut with surprise, a surfeit of *¡Madre de Dios!* and *¡Dios mío!* their voices reacting to an orthodoxy of pleasure, it was the real thing, wasn't it, absolutely authentic, in every respect, and Wilber Eduardo, it can't be true but I'm reading it, so it must be true, José Matías, you can bet your life it's true, *mi hermano,* proud of the cooperation on the part of the citizenry, and the Center for Justice and Accountability, on April 11, 2013, announcing for all the world to see, the release, at last, by the Justice Department, a document, and the exact words of immigration judge James K. Grim's ruling, ordering the deportation of General Juan Humberto Reyes Vehemente (hereinafter Respondent) commander of the Salvadoran National Guard between 1979 and 1983, to El Salvador.

The broad outline of the ruling, known since the judge issued it in February 2012, and reaffirming it in August, his reasoning and supporting documentation, the breadth, depth and scope of it all, the decision, a finding ordering the former general's removal, everything remaining a secret on account of the Justice Department, controlling immigration courts, which declined to release the information until now, and today, not very long ago, it felt like yesterday, it was in their hands, thanks to their cousin Luz, the Flores brothers, José Matías and Wilber Eduardo, trembling with excitement at the discovery that turned their eyes to saucers.

Extract:

VI. Conclusion

In summary, upon careful review of the entirety of the record, for the specific reasons discussed above, the Court sustains all the allegations in the charging documents, and finds Respondent removable pursuant to section 237(a)(4)(D) of the Act as an alien described in INA § 212(a)(3)(E)(iii)(II), on the following independent bases:

1) Respondent assisted or otherwise participated in the extrajudicial killings of Manuel Toledo and Vinicio Bazzaglia;

2) Respondent assisted or otherwise participated in the extrajudicial killings of American churchwomen Ita Ford, Maura Clarke, Dorothy Kazel, and Jean Donovan;

3) Respondent assisted or otherwise participated in the extrajudicial killings of Michael Hammer, Mark Pearlman, and José Rodofo Viera at the Sheraton Hotel;

4) Respondent assisted or otherwise participated in the extrajudicial killings of at least 16 Salvadoran peasants at Las Hojas, Sansonate;

5) Respondent assisted or otherwise participated in the extrajudicial killings of three individuals found on February 1, 1988 at Puerta del Diablo;

6) Respondent assisted or otherwise participated in the extrajudicial killings of ten individuals in the (b)(6) area; and

7) Respondent assisted or otherwise participated in the extrajudicial killings of countless civilians committed by the Salvadoran Armed Forces and Salvadoran National Guard while under Respondent's command.
In addition, upon careful review of the entirety of the record, for the specific reasons discussed above, the Court finds Respondent removable pursuant to section 237(a)(4)(D) of the Act as an alien described in NA §212(a)(3)(E)(iii)(I), on the following independent bases:

1) Respondent assisted or otherwise participated in the torture of (b)(6)

2) Respondent assisted or otherwise participated in the torture of (b)(6) (b)(6) and

3) Respondent assisted or otherwise participated in the torture of countless unnamed individuals, tortured by the Salvadoran Armed Forces and Salvadoran National Guard while under Respondent's command.

José Matías and Wilber Eduardo, the Flores brothers, bruised from beatings and banging around in the back of a truck, a slap in the face and a kick in the balls, their first encounter with the *cuilios,* then the helicopter ride, on their way to El Paraíso, a garrison, before reaching the National Guard headquarters in the big city, scratched and bruised but standing, and now, after a couple of days at headquarters, a room four by four feet — they didn't have a yardstick or a ruler to measure it, their feet, maybe, but they were swollen and dirty and bleeding, and it wasn't easy to walk on them, the Flores brothers, separate rooms, not the best hotel in the country, caged and suffocated by the length of their own arms and legs — you could hear the traffic in the street at midday, or it was screams from other men and women, a loud harsh piercing cry, like screeching tires, a lot of cuts, slices of skin shaved off with a machete, not enough to kill anyone, just a little skinning, and lesions and track marks from electric shock treatments, then vomiting tortillas and beans in a corner of the cell, and pain, plenty of that went along with it.

Not enough room for both of them, they shared everything except the cell they slept in, but standing in the corridor, catching a glimpse, making eye contact, maybe in adjacent cells, and the smell of someone shitting themselves, it wasn't me you motherfucker! crawling, kicked and cursed, life sinking in the shit, but without giving up, and the weariness of absolute death that doesn't come, count with your fingers while they still work, with the national anthem every morning, and cramps in the lower belly where they hit them, one at a time, shitting in their pants, you can sleep in your own shit, *culero,* or wipe it on your brother's face.

José Matías, shivering and sweating, a body temperature out of its mind, rising and falling, José Matías crawling on all fours in front of Wilber Eduardo, his brother, trembling without cold, the Flores brothers — what was it, what was it — with blood running out of their ears, they couldn't hear the shouting but they felt the blows landing on them as they scurried around on the dirty floor, an enormous sensation of calm invaded them, after the panic there was only calm, and a unanimous sensation of renunciation, together, of impotence and resignation, that for today, until they were brought back to their cells, the room of four by four feet, there was nothing one could do to help the other, or help themselves, and once separated, there was nothing left but to listen through the walls for the other's shortened breath, at least they were breathing, pulling themselves together, that was it, breathing heavily now, and then to sleep, break-ing into a snore, to be awakened in the obscured night by the crying out of another victim and another torturer, whose voices merged in absurd unison.

And they were heading in the direction of the town of Lajas y Canoas, an elevation of fifteen hundred feet above sea level, uncultivated land with most of its natural vegetation intact, but Lajas y Canoas wasn't the Flores brothers' des-tination, not on this journey, the pickup navigating the road both good and bad that was taking them in a northerly direction, toward Lajas y Canoas, a town without many people, a small population, maybe they'd see a woman cov-ered with a shawl to protect herself from the sun, a boy holding her hand, the index finger of his other hand stuck straight in his mouth, a dusty, untidy-looking cat in the shade of a tree pulling feathers off a dead bird — wait until you get there before deciding what you'll see — and the Flores brothers, they weren't stopping in Lajas y Canoas, but continuing further north and slightly east, the pickup towing the wind behind them, and the *cadejos,* watching the sky from where they were lying in the bed of the truck as it flew by above the tropical savanna.

José Matías and Wilber Eduardo and the *cadejos*, they were all together on their way to San Ildefonso, a population of maybe ten thousand, where Graciela Menéndez, at her parent's house, preparing for what, she didn't know, but she'd felt she had to do something because she'd had a vision, and with it a question hanging in the air, right above her, day and night, and she believed it for years, it was something she couldn't put a name to, but she was convinced that whatever it was she was going to have to live through it, it was her fate, or that someone else she knew was going to experience what she'd seen as a sign, an apparition, not once but many times, as clear to her as if it had come out of a dream and sat down in front of her, she hadn't noticed an ominous augury, but she'd seen it, she'd had her eyes open, Graciela Menéndez, always rubbing herself with lotion, dry skin, maybe eczema, atopic dermatitis, daydreaming and premonitions, and when she rubbed lotion on her body she fell into a trance, having visions or portents, that was Graciela Menéndez, and so she'd buried a talisman in the backyard of her parent's house, an inanimate object worshiped for its magical powers, and it was that talisman the Flores brothers wanted now more than ever, a talisman buried in the backyard of a house in the town of San Ildefonso.

But being on the road, traveling at high speed, as fast as the pickup and the roads allowed, which wasn't very fast, didn't really take them away from what they were afraid of, José Matías and Wilber Eduardo, the Flores brothers, and José Matías, driving, he kept on smoking, gripping the wheel with a fist but showing nothing on his face for his brother to worry about, while Wilber Eduardo, breathing heavily without making a sound, slowly, to calm himself, like he'd read in books, but all the time praying, wishing he could light a candle to San Martín de Porres to protect them both, the saint who is black like the night, our protection, San Martín de Porres, in addition to the magic dogs, who must be traveling with us, but I don't see them, God protect us.

Wilber Eduardo said a prayer which he repeated countless times, his brother heard nothing, it was a silent prayer, but Wilber Eduardo, moving his lips, and José Matías, out of the corner of an eye, peripheral vision like nobody else, even while driving the pickup, a cigarette dangling from a corner of his mouth, what are you worrying about, *mi hermano,* we're headed where we've got to go in order to get ourselves out of this hole, it's like we're forced into a tight corner, and we can't even see what we're fighting, like when the cemetery in Mario's village was destroyed, where both his grandparents were buried, nothing was left but a pile of rocks, and then Mario told us, "Not even the dead are safe from this war."

We'll find what we need, *mi hermano,* in the backyard of Graciela Menéndez's parents' house, and together, with the magic dogs, our protectors, we'll get help, because I understand that when all is said and done, our situation is part of the struggle against mysteries we know nothing about, and we shouldn't complain, we're fighting for a better world for everyone, in our own way, and that's why, in difficult moments like these, we've got to find the courage to go on, José Matías, *¿me entiendes?* so I see that you're right, and together we'll rid ourselves of what scared us, ghost or no ghost, which will give the same courage — *un regalo,* a gift — to other people in our country faced every day with a fearful memory that jumps out at them from behind a *jocote* tree or appears above the shrubs at the side of the road.

Wilber Eduardo, happy with himself for having found courage — reaching for a twelve-ounce can when there wasn't a twelve-ounce can of Kolashampan Bravo under the seat — happy with himself and grinning like a Cheshire cat on account of having found the right words to tell his brother he supported him, through and through, wholly, fully and entirely, without condition, one hundred percent perfect solidarity between siblings, bringing them together in the name of a cause they couldn't avoid even if they wanted to avoid it, it stood there like a fat pillar of stone that wouldn't budge even if they dynamited it, the fright they'd got, that was it, together, José Matías and Wilber Eduardo, the Flores brothers, hiding behind a boulder, just before running into a neighing horse that raised and lowered its head, nodding at them like it was agreeing with something, maybe with what they were thinking, the two of them, at the same time, being frightened is a full-time job, a vocation that never ends, and with it, the bleak future they were facing now.

José Matías, an exhalation from behind the wheel, a little relief, and a slap with the open palm of his hand on his brother's shoulder — it was a reach on account of the width of the cab — don't hold your breath, breathe easy, we're almost there, and when we're through, maybe we'll have sent the ghost to La Bermeja, in the capital, where it belongs, to a poor grave behind the poor, cream-colored walls, with all the poor crosses made of poor dry branches, but most likely it'll end up in *El Cementerio de Los Ilustres,* back to where it came from, with the rich — the rich have the luxury of taking their time before settling down, even when they're dead — and Wilber Eduardo, nodding his head, you're right, *mi hermano,* it just depends on whose ghost it is, and in any case, it doesn't matter where the dead are buried, everything ends there, we can't shit on the honorable people who earned us the choice between heaven and hell.

What I wouldn't give for a tamarind juice, I'm so thirsty, and Wilber Eduardo, scratching a scab on his face where he'd picked a pimple without squeezing it and now it was an old-money centavo-size red spot on his face that itched once he'd been in the hot sun that dried it out, don't touch it, *mi hermano,* and José Matías, after looking at him out of the corner of his eye — he didn't miss a thing — it'll leave a scar, he turned the wheel of the pickup to avoid the dried-up corpse of a flattened Tacuazín lying in the middle of the road, Wilber Eduardo, and what's a scar after what we've been through, José Matías? because there are scars and then there are scars, and we've got plenty, on the skin, and beneath the surface that cut straight to the heart of our souls.

Wilber Eduardo, turning his head, looking right at his brother, what I'm afraid of, what I mean is, all the signs, on the road and elsewhere, no left turn, no right turn, no U-turn, do not enter, what comes out of my well-oiled brain is that life is a wonderful thing when we're on the road, as long as we're far away from what troubles us, oppresses us, burdens us, torments us, *mi hermano,* there are things that are never meant to be known, and I quote: "the mystery of the world is a world of mystery," so I don't give a whore's hard shit for anything but getting out of this jam — it's like we were on a bender to end all benders last night, a real *¡zumba, mi hermano!* and we're suffering a hangover that makes us see things that aren't there.

The sun's rays shone on the windshield and would've blinded them with its glare except for their Ray-Bans and the angle of the rays themselves. It was a persistent sun that didn't seem to have changed much since they were hiding behind the big boulder with the neighing horse standing not ten feet away from them, Wilber Eduardo, his eyes shut behind the lenses of his sunglasses, seeing there on the lids of his eyes, like two movie screens projecting one expanded CinemaScope picture for him, a small village on a mountain full of snakes and iguanas, where a man learned all the things a man has to learn to survive in the country, Wilber Eduardo, a tear forming at the corner of an eye, rolling silently down his cheek, it was a ghost town now, bombed, knocked out — including the disappeared, the tortured, and the dead — destroyed by fighting between guerillas and the army, and José Matías, don't pay attention to it, *mi hermano,* we've seen it all before, life's too short, and we both know that's a fact.

After they were beaten up, the Flores brothers, José Matías and Wilber Eduardo, were thrown into the same truck at the same time, and then flown, together, in the helicopter to El Paraíso, the Flores brothers, José Matías and Wilber Eduardo, standing in the garrison, weak legs but standing, a poorly lighted, dingy room with the smell of burned tobacco, cheap aftershave, they were looking around but seeing nothing on account of a couple of blackened eyes and blurred vision, a worn-out chair with dark varnish rubbed off its arms and legs, there was nothing like freedom there in that barracks room, standing in front of a sergeant with stained and broken teeth, heavy black boots laced up and his military trousers tucked neatly into them.

José Matías and Wilber Eduardo, trying to gather their thoughts, it was a windy day up there in their heads, the crashing waves, the interior stream running dry of ideas, a lot of scraps of writing that looked like notes they'd been taking of things to do — there was nothing they could do but try to keep body and soul together — their thoughts were blowing around up there between their ears, Wilber Eduardo bleeding from one of them, a warm, sticky trail of blood running toward his chin, or not running at all, dried to his skin turning blue and black, black and blue, and José Matías, with a bruised or broken cheekbone and a loose tooth.

José Matías, his vision clearing, unclouded, looking at the guard, thinking of what he'd like to say to his brother, did I tell you, *mi hermano,* I dreamt I had a toothless mouth, *¡puchica!* it was a real nightmare, at first there were only a few of them left inside, a gapping hole of a mouth with to-bacco-stained stumps, like this asshole with his stained and broken teeth, then they crumbled and turned to calcium dust, resting like a lump of paste in my mouth before I swallowed them, having mustered enough saliva to wash it all down my throat — then, no teeth at all, but José Matías and Wilber Eduardo, they couldn't say a word, so Wilber Eduardo, his brother, wouldn't hear about his dream, not now, maybe another day if they lived to see it, and the guard, reading his mind, a shout made of mangled words, no talking — you shit-for-brains, and you, turning to Wilber Eduardo, you shit-for-luck, what're you looking at, I'll gouge your eyes out with a spoon! and the Flores brothers suddenly felt the urge to commend themselves to God, but there wasn't a church in sight.

For a few seconds, before they were separated and put into individual cells, a confused sensation invaded them, they weren't sure if they were awake or dreaming, until the intense burning spreading outward like rays of hot sunlight exploded in their bellies at almost the same time, a delay of less than a second between blows from the guard, another guard joined them, then a swift kick for each of them, dragging the Flores brothers by their shirt collars, frayed and blood-stained, throwing them each into their respective rooms — not the best hotel in the country — José Matías and Wilber Eduardo, sobbing without meaning to give anything away, José Matías, the sons-of-bitches, I can't show them anything, no sign of weakness, no screams and moans, and Wilber Eduardo, no howling, no protruding eyes and purple tongue, nothing, *¡pendejada!* they regretted it like it was a sin, their suffering in plain view for all the world and these murderers to see on their faces, and the Flores brothers, together, saying to themselves, at the same time with the same words, fate plays with us, a shared thought before crumpling to the cell floor.

You've pissed yourself, José Matías pulling to the side of the road, what does it mean, *mi hermano,* but trouble, are you okay? maybe a little walk in the sun, and José Matías, getting out and walking around the pickup, opening the passenger door, helping his brother get out of the cab, stained trousers, wet with urine, if you needed to stop you could've told me, but Wilber Eduardo, ashamed, lowering his head, it wasn't that, it was fright, something that scared me, and I couldn't hold it, *mi hermano,* and that's the sad truth, I've got a weak bladder, ever since, well, it's obvious, isn't it? we've got our cross to bear, and we aren't the only ones, it felt like the weight of *Las Chiches* was crushing me, and it wasn't our mother's tit, either, I was suckling death itself, the weight pushing out what was in my bladder, it pressed hard on my balls and I had to piss, José Matías, so thank you for getting me out of the truck and into the sun.

The life-giving Lempa wasn't so far away from where they were standing, they couldn't see it, it was too far away to be seen, but its lively spirit rose into the sky and traveled from its banks, flowing to them on a light wind like the water itself, while the sun dried Wilber Eduardo's trousers and his brother smoked another cigarette, it was the Río

Lempa calling to them, or reminding them that it was there, waiting for them and the moment when they were ready to join it like a lake might wait for mountain water to fill it, and the river's spirit sang with a voice that made them think of the Sunday mass broadcast by YSAX, the two brothers in the kitchen, huddled together, with their elbows on their knees, black coffee steaming hot in two mugs on the kitchen table, they were listening, not to Circuito YSR, YSEB or YSKL — although sometimes, in those days, they listened to Radio Venceremos, jammed, changing frequency, jammed, changing frequency again — but always listening to the Monsignor on YSAX, and José Matías and Wilber Eduardo, the words flowing over them from the radio, from the Metropolitan Cathedral, reassuring in tragic and violent times that were now behind them, the Flores brothers, a revolver waving around in their faces, a memory as detailed as the time on Wilber Eduardo's watch, a birthday present from Gustavo, the Flores brothers, a couple of living dead men, swinging in a hammock, thrown over the saddle of a horse, dumped in a ditch by the side of the road, not *la Carretera Panamericana*, not now, but José Matías and Wilber Eduardo, they weren't free from the ghosts of the past.

Wilber Eduardo's trousers were almost dry, his shame had evaporated with the urine, composed of water and the jar of Miguel's Changungas' syrup he'd swallowed thirstily, a belly full of nance fruit, after fear had choked him, *Las Chiches* suffocating him, weighing him down, strangling the body's functions and squeezing out of his bladder a stream of piss that stained his trousers and scarred his thigh with the message it carried, praying it wasn't a portent of what was to come, Wilber Eduardo, shaking one leg, loosening the tense muscles and relaxing the joints to allow the flow of blood to make its way to his toes, José Matías crushing the butt of a Delta Red, not *mentolado* — he couldn't stand them — trampling on it in the dirt, let's get going, you're all right now, aren't you, it was just a fright, and we haven't eaten lunch.

In a village that wasn't a village but half a dozen adobe houses — as much of the village as they could see — situated on either side of the road that was a secondary highway running north, each house with a large front porch, mud-brick houses lining a main street that was the continuation of a highway, a few stacks of wood cut for stoves next to the houses beside the road, a small grocery store with a bakery in back next to the last house at the end of a row of three, like the store was a late but not unimportant thought, and Wilber Eduardo, food and supplies, we've all got to have them, so there's bound to be something to eat and drink, a short beer, beans and tortillas, what do you say? let a tired man stretch his legs, come as you are, and a well to draw water, where are we anyway? and José Matías pulled off the road, switched off the engine but kept the pickup facing in the same direction they were headed, the Flores brothers sitting in the cab, let's take our time, what's the hurry, and Wilber Eduardo, aren't we going to eat? José Matías, there isn't a soul in sight, *mi hermano,* and two pairs of eyes behind sunglasses looking at everything around them, suspicion or just the habit, and spying the low trees separating the houses, providing a little shade from the sun.

They got out of the truck and stood together in front of the warm engine in the still, warm air, a dog barked, ran out from behind the general store and headed toward them, the Flores brothers looking at the dog that didn't resemble one of the *cadejos* riding in the bed of the truck, but a scrawny dog, its tongue hanging out, panting, thirsty, it stopped halfway down the road, stood staring at them, and then there was movement in one of the trees, a child perched on a branch, wearing an orange T-shirt, arm dangling in the air with a finger pointing at the dusty earth, in his enthusiasm to discover other worlds, *cabañuelas,* the science of interpreting the movement of celestial bodies, maybe forecasting the weather, a child looking at a constellation in an enchanted projection on the earth of the sky above 13°30′N 89°W —the adobe houses weren't directly under the sky belonging to the capital city, but a boy, not more than eleven years old, wearing an orange T-shirt, saw the constellation and dropped down to the northern part of it from the branch of the tree and landed in the middle of Ursa Minor — it was the Smaller Bear, +74°4′40″ — even if it wasn't winter, the boy, in all seasons, winter, spring, summer, autumn, the boy always saw that constellation from the branch of his tree, and when he jumped down, maybe he landed right on Polaris.

As fast as he could run the boy headed toward the Flores brothers, José Matías and Wilber Eduardo, standing without moving, not a breath or shiver, and the boy wearing an orange T-shirt fell to his knees and wrapped his arms around Wilber Eduardo's legs, whose trousers were dry from the heat of the sun, and the boy, a firm grip with fingers entwined, his shoulders rising and falling, Wilber Eduardo's knees brought together in his grasp, and José Matías, wondering if the boy was weeping or laughing.

Then the Flores brothers looked away from the boy and up at the sky, a flight of cormorants over the adobe houses, over the near-distant Pan-American Highway, CA1, José Matías and Wilber Eduardo, and the boy in the orange T-shirt hugging Wilber Eduardo's legs, and the flight of cormorants wasn't a symbol of avarice and dishonesty, not anymore, not any longer, but another sign on their journey, a good omen, like the confident and optimistic words spoken by a loving mother, when they were children, telling them before tucking them into bed that the little rocks blown into their garden from the volcano were each an inspiration because they traveled so far, and the noble, patrician, honorable and upright bougainvilleas — one-two-three, I crown you — the banana trees and the nance with its yellow flowers and spoon-shaped petals — bright yellow before they turned orange and red as they matured, don't blink or you'll miss it, an imprecise and finally precise something — they're evidence of God's wish to cultivate our dreams because, you see, *mis hijitos,* they're growing in our garden, giving us beauty and something sweet to eat, the expression of God's love for his children — Agnus Dei, qui tollis peccáta mundi, dona nobis pacem — and we're all God's children, *mis angelitos.*

So Wilber Eduardo lifted the boy from his knees and the ground and carried him in his arms, José Matías walking beside them, no cigarette for now, but an open pack in his shirt pocket, the Flores brothers and the little boy, together, hearing music, it was floating toward them in the air, coming from an open window, from somewhere nearby, a song of the Pipils, descendants of the Aztecs of México, maybe coming from one of the houses, but not the store, definitely not, the music wasn't near enough to be coming from the store, then hearing another short song, the accordion music and singing of Francisco Tepas, and at last, on the threshold, so to speak, Francisco Tepas' accordion, playing a simple instrumental, a kind of waltz, "Me duele," that drew them to a front porch, the boy wearing an orange T-shirt pointing all the way, not kicking and screaming, it was almost like he'd been waiting for them, the Flores brothers, and beyond the front porch, only a few steps, the house where the boy lived with his mother.

What's your mother's name, *jovencito?* and the boy, looking up at Wilber Eduardo, a grin from ear to ear, Dolores, she's called Mama Lola, and the Flores brothers throwing both of them a smile, the door shutting noisily behind them, and the boy's mother, Dolores, making tortillas, maybe five millimeters thick and ten centimeters in diameter, and heating up leftover beans and rice, steam rising from the pot, stirring them with a wooden spoon, and the smell of food in the kitchen swirling around them, filling the room and making them dizzy — they were so hungry it knocked the sense out of them — warming beans and rice and frying tortillas of *maicillo,* a wonderful odor impregnating the walls and the ceiling and the floor, until the boy, wriggling, fidgeting, and climbing down from the arms that held him, released gently from Wilber Eduardo's grasp, excited, waving to the Flores brothers, José Matías and Wilber Eduardo, the boy shouting, *cheros!* — with respect — come on, let's eat! moving little wooden stools around the table for the Flores brothers, his guests, and for his mother, Mama Lola, to sit on after she put the steaming bowl of beans and rice and the plate of warm tortillas on the table in front of them, the boy filling a couple of glasses with shaved ice and pouring mango syrup over the ice, giving the Flores brothers each a glass.

"Let's get down to business," said Mama Lola after everyone was served, "what are you doing here? Nobody comes here, they mostly leave — for San Vicente, or maybe Sensunte-peque, where's there's nothing, really, but it's a neat and clean little town, do you know Parque Luciano Hernández — *poeta y político*?"

José Matías and Wilber Eduardo, each holding a spoonful of beans and rice in front of their mouths, she'd started talking out of a clear blue sky, they'd been sitting there in silence, and Wilber Eduardo felt the boy gently kicking him beneath the table, or kicking one of the legs of the wooden stool, affectionately, a little nervous maybe, but they were a family, resembling one, the length of time it took to eat lunch, and at the same time, the same words, both of them: "No, we don't know it, but the name, Luciano Hernández, yes, maybe the name."

They shoveled spoonfuls of beans and rice in their mouths, but not so fast that they couldn't taste it, the Flores broth-ers, chewing them thoroughly, but they were so hungry, and the tortillas, warm, freshly made, a satisfaction bringing memories of their mother's cooking, not a lot of food but delicious, the aroma, and their innocence, but they'd lived through the worst of it, the civil war, and it was today, and they were sitting with strangers who invited them to a meal, a boy and his mother, Dolores.

"Mama, can I ask them? Can I say something to the *cheros* — with respect, of course — you know, when my mouth isn't full, I wasn't brought up that way," raising another spoonful full of hot beans and rice to his lips, blowing on them to cool them off, chewing and swallowing them as he waited for Mama Lola to answer him, and the boy in his purity smiled at his mother.

"Yes, Elio, you can ask them whatever you want, always be polite, and they can always say no."

"Your name's Elio, *jovencito?*" and José Matías, draping himself in a cloak of memories, a childhood friend, the same nickname, but he was killed by the National Guard, and José Matías, smiling at the boy as he stirred his plate of beans and rice with his spoon, "What kind of name is Elio?" ruffling the hair on the boy's head, he turned to his brother and said, "You remember Elio, *mi hermano?*" and Wilber Eduardo, whistling softly, shut his eyes.

"Rogelio, my name's Rogelio, but my mother calls me Elio."

The boy, taking another spoonful of beans and rice, blowing away the steam rising from it, almost trembling with excitement, he had something to say and if he didn't say it he'd burst, his eyes were big and bright as he chewed and swallowed his food, then the boy in the orange T-shirt, putting his spoon on the table, looking up at the Flores brother, and Dolores resting her arm around his shoulders, encouraging him, José Matías and Wilber Eduardo, feeling stillness without seeing it, listening to the warm air buzzing like flies around them, the Flores brothers looked up from their plates of beans and rice and tortillas and saw the boy, saw Rogelio staring at them with wide-open eyes.

"You were captured, and they took you to the Capital, didn't they? There was nothing left of the vibrant, yellow sun that looked like a huge gold coin, not after that, it was a dark spot, ugly, a stain you'd never wipe off your soul — no thanks to them, were you prisoner of the soldiers? Of the National Guard? Darkness or daylight, it doesn't matter, they're synonymous with kidnapping and arrest, torture and death, did they beat you, then pick you up and throw you in a truck? I can see it right away, with any man or woman who comes through our village, past our house, they don't have to talk to me, not a word between us, but I know they've been tortured, captured by soldiers, all I have to do is look out the window, here, you see it? I just look out that window at them riding through our village, a horse, a burro, in a car, a four-wheel drive, on foot, any kind of transportation, and I know right away what's happened to them, all misery and despair, nothing like a wedding or the birth of a child, no, I never see anything like that — only sorrow, suffering and death; Mama Lola says I've got a gift and it's a gift given me by God, and what I see when I see it is always right, maybe I ought to respect it, but it gives me a very sad feeling, *cheros,* you can imagine how sad I am, not only for the people I see passing our house, but accompanying all those who have suffered are the souls, the ghosts of bodies and even the bones of the dead, so many of them that they can't fit in my mind, so sometimes I stay in my room, the window closed no matter how hot the sun is beating down on the roof of our little house, in my room, over there, with my eyes shut and weeping, without making a sound because I don't want to frighten Mama Lola, I don't want to make her feel as sad as I am sad."

José Matías and Wilber Eduardo, they were speechless — those words that speak realities, those words that speak truths — grains of cooked rice and a few beans sitting on their tongues without the Flores brothers being able to swallow them, it was their turn to have bulging eyes, less bright than the boy's eyes, but moist with emotion, and respect for the power he was given by God — whose God, do you still believe in him? — to see within them, to see so deeply within them that he, an uninitiated boy in a small village, knew their story.

"And what do you see now, Elio?" Wilber Eduardo unable to take another bite of food until he heard what the boy had to say, and his brother, José Matías, his head bowed, hands folded, "May God save us from what we've seen and been through," the words barely audible, they weren't alone, everyone had more than a fair share of suffering, and so many dead — the brutality of the soldiers and guardsmen — but the Flores brothers, it didn't take their pain and fear away, counting victims living and dead until they couldn't count anymore, it wasn't enough, my capacity to recognize my incapacity, José Matías and Wilber Eduardo, thinking it but not saying a word, because inside and out, from head to toe, skin and guts, yes, the boy's right, we're stained for life by the poisonous ink they injected in our veins.

Dolores raised her spoon full of beans and rice, chewing them slowly, looking at nothing with her eyes fixed on the tabletop directly in front of her, head tilted slightly downward, looking like she was thinking about something other than the food she was eating, and then Dolores, Mama Lola to her son, go ahead, say it, encouraging an answer to Wilber Eduardo's question, she washed the beans and rice down with a swallow from a glass of shaved ice, flavored with something that wasn't mango syrup, maybe papaya, and the ice was melting in the heat, the Flores brothers raised their glasses, a lot of melted ice and mango, to quench their thirst, not because of the heat but because their mouths were dry from remembering everything at once, no taking a breather, the memories were flooding in, and so they swallowed a couple of mouthfuls of *minuta,* a flavored ice drink, to refresh themselves.

Rogelio, another spoonful of beans and rice, boiled beans that were seasoned with Hidalgo chili peppers, or maybe *Diente de perro* from Nicaragua, and the rice, too, the smell filling his nostrils, he chewed slowly, keeping his mouth shut, letting the seconds tick without insisting, he wanted to know if he was right, not what really happened to them, wanting to know if his gift was still intact, but he didn't want to rush them, José Matías and Wilber Eduardo, *nuestros cheros,* let them take their time, he told himself, it can't be pleasant, and it's really terrible, maybe to think about it at all is the worst thing for them today, or any day, to remember the things they're remembering now, and anyway, by the look on their faces, I know that I'm right.

The boy's questions floated for more than a minute and then became a part of the zone of the forgotten, or not so forgotten but avoided for as long as it took the Flores brothers to settle down from memories that were more real than reality itself, Wilber Eduardo, so what if reality forces us to go on, it's making me sick to my stomach, *mi hermano,* causing dryness of the mouth and fearful trembling, you know the symptoms, and you look as bad as I do, José Matías, *sé fuerte,* but maybe they can't see it, maybe they don't know what to look for, *sacarlo,* it's misery thinking about it, and the question, you were captured, and they took you to the Capital, didn't they? — that first question from the boy in the orange T-shirt, Rogelio — was enough to make them stagger backward, trip and fall down in the past, straight into the moment the soldiers threw them in the truck, a slap in the face and a kick in the balls, like it was yesterday.

It's more than we can stand to go through it again, and the other thing, that horse, nodding its head, a horse without a rider, and the ghost or monster, something out of a Mexican horror movie, if it weren't for the magic dogs, the *cadejos,* even if they couldn't see them, they weren't far away, resting in the shade of an evergreen shrub, it wasn't so long ago, and we can't forget why we're on the road, Graciela Menéndez, and a talisman in the backyard of her parents' house, an object worshiped for its magical powers, *mi hermano,* remember? and Wilber Eduardo, you don't have to remind me, José Matías.

They couldn't swallow another bite of what they were trying to digest of their memories, their stomachs were full — their backs were crushed, souls caved in — and now, looking at Elio and Dolores, forcing a smile as an offering of peace to the boy, maybe he could see how uncomfortable they were after the questions he'd asked them, the Flores brothers, but there's nothing to say, nothing to tell you that would make it clear to you, Elio, because it's our story, beyond the consideration of science, the pain and suffering stop with us, and anything else, like telling you what happened, is just an anecdote for the history books, so what's the point? is it our history or is it our story? but okay, yes, you're right, you *were* right, what you saw when you looked at us, perched on a branch, your arm dangling in the air with a finger pointing at the dusty earth — it looked like you were examining a constellation in an enchanted projection on the earth of the sky above us — your enthusiasm to discover other worlds, we were standing next to the pickup, and you, jumping down and running toward us, hugging my brother's legs, and the dog barking, well, what you saw when you saw us was the truth, but we aren't here to perpetuate by words a sad tradition of torture, suffering, disappearance and death, *jovencito.*

Dolores, eating heartily, listening, encouraging her son to finish his beans and rice, another tortilla of *maicillo,* you've heard all you need to hear, and you haven't had enough to eat, *hijo mío,* the gift is still yours, it belongs to you as a gift from God, but now you've got to finish what's on your plate, and another tortilla.

The Flores brothers, shaking it off, athletes of a certain kind of pain — bearing the mark of the color of having undergone something bad or unpleasant, but never hardened over by indifference and antipathy — José Matías and Wilber Eduardo, discomfort really, and on the Scoville scale, a hot one, a rating of around 350,000 units, but no tears, they're fit enough to leave it for now, the questions Rogelio asked, and in front of them, the plate of beans and rice and tortillas, they weren't as hungry as they'd been but wanted to eat anyway, a spoonful of beans and rice, a mouthful of mango-flavored shaved ice that had melted in the heat, another spoonful of beans and rice, and the Flores brothers, Rogelio and Dolores, together, sitting at the table, were quietly eating their lunch again.

Five minutes passed, and Rogelio, hesitating, but sure of himself, Rogelio, the complete salvation and uplifting of man by the light of the Gospel, the most important goal we've got as human beings making our home in the same land on this our earth, working together, and propelling each other forward, without forgetting our past, and every one of us — *está bien yuca* — our brothers and sisters, mothers and fathers, cousins, aunts and uncles — I know, we all know it, I've got my head in the clouds — okay, but there's at least one in any family, take a look around, who knows or is related to someone who's been arrested, tortured, maybe killed — El Mozote, Arcatao and Río Sumpul, El Calabozo and Río Amatitán, on account of *Batallón Atlacatl,* or *Batallón Ramón Belloso,* two of six *Batallones de Infantería de Reacción Inmediata,* BIRIs, and among the BIRIs, the Atlacatl Battalion was the worst when it came to violating human rights, a strategy of mass murder, killing by zone, sweep-and-destroy operations, that's what they called them — so what you've gone through, *cheros,* what all the others like you have gone through, it's enough to make the world cry — sure, it was a long time ago, you've grown past your own suffering, but who can forget it? it's going on in some country somewhere right now — so what's left for us but faith, and a little "With my gaze set on God and on you," for Monsignor Romero, okay, but he's dead, so rising above our fate, bathed in light that is a light of an evangelical and moral nature, and then Rogelio, taking another bite of his tortilla, a spoonful of beans and rice, a pause in his discourse to chew and swallow his meal, while José Matías and Wilber Eduardo, eating and listening but finding it hard to believe that a boy Elio's age could say what he's saying without losing the innocence of a child, or maybe thanks to it.

And Dolores, his mother, Mama Lola, smiling, she'd heard it before, a dozen guests for lunch and a dozen times she'd heard Elio tell them the same thing, a fundamental view, her son calling attention to Monsignor Romero, maybe something he'd read in school, *la voz de los sin voz,* a necessary expression of compassion, nothing forced, it was his desire to say it, always to say it, and to say it over and over again, it was something that carried Rogelio along in order to be able to live with his gift or he'd depart this life today on account of the pain he absorbed into his bloodstream, gifts of pain from passersby, riding through the village, a horse, a burro, in a car, a four-wheel drive, on foot, any kind of transportation, and an invitation to lunch, each and every one of them who'd suffered at the hands of the soldiers or guardsmen, they left behind a part of themselves, their past which never left them, morning, noon, and night, and each visit deposited a sorrow with the weight of the world alongside the empty plates of beans and rice they left on the table after sharing a meal with them.

So the Flores brothers, together, the same word at the same time, *¡Cabal!* slang for *exacto,* they agreed in essence to everything Rogelio was saying, even if it shot past them like a dart, words out of a child's mouth, a dart as poisonous as their memories, they'd dodged it, but a near miss, it was more than they wanted to feel, at this moment, with an assignment to complete, an overpowering obligation, a job lying ahead of them, they needed their strength, it was a task they'd appointed themselves, the task of acquiring the talisman in the backyard of Graciela Menéndez's parents' house, José Matías and Wilber Eduardo, their eyes confirmed there was work to be done — no theories and no ideas — taking the right measures to chase away the ghost they'd seen rising out of nowhere not so far from the *tempisque,* and plenty of other trees, the *tihuilote* trees or a White Sapote.

The Flores brothers, excusing themselves, José Matías, I need a smoke, taking a cigarette out of a pack of Delta Reds in his shirt pocket, his brother, Wilber Eduardo, getting up with him, timed to the second, a movement fluid and synchronized in order to accompany his brother out to the porch, a few words not spoken — Wilber Eduardo, in Náhuatl, the language of the Aztecs, *Intlacamo ximocahuaz, nipehuaz nichoca,* if you don't stop, I'll start to cry, and a reassuring voice replying, *Macahmo ximochocti,* do not cry — while his brother dragged on his cigarette, Wilber Eduardo, leaning closer to his brother, the figure of the hero helps to bridge the gap between myth and history, and José Matías adding — words anyone could hear passing between them — the hero's usually a man who's lived on earth, *mi hermano,* with a definite lifespan, beginning with his birth and ending with his death or disappearance, José Matías exhaling a cloud of smoke, looking at Wilber Eduardo, and Wilber Eduardo, then it wasn't a hero, that can't be what we saw — you remember what it looked like — it was merely a ghost, our past, at our heels, José Matías nodded his head, agreeing, but a frown somewhere behind the faint smile, and the sun leaning out of its heights in the middle of the sky, small houses and trees and shrubs throwing shadows like great stones, an early part of the afternoon settling in on the village where they'd enjoyed a meal with Rogelio and his mother.

José Matías, we'll have to get going now so the color will return to our faces — if you could only see yourself, *mi hermano* — driving makes us sing and singing drives away evil, I read it somewhere, but I'm not in the mood, what do you say? and no whistling, that's the worst, sometimes our bodies are so scared they're obstacles to the spirit, *mi hermano,* sunlight draws out the things to come, so let's hurry, our almost all-consuming fear takes the shine off everything, and Wilber Eduardo, forcing a smile, enough to hold him upright beside his duty to the job lying ahead of them, and

José Matías, it all adds up to what we do with our fear, *mi hermano,* rid ourselves of the smell of the tomb, the sky has eyes that are watching us, and Wilber Eduardo, and are watching over us; they went back in the house to say good-bye to Rogelio and Dolores.

José Matías and Wilber Eduardo would've liked to sleep, a siesta after their meal, tired and full of beans and tortillas, but a siesta wasn't going to get them where they were going, no rest for the weary, or for the Flores brothers, places to go and things to see — a not very casual observance, to break the backs of devils, to banish ghosts torturing them each with a crippling affliction of the nervous system — the hermeneutic phase was closed, they'd opened the practical phase, so there were places to go, things to be done, other skies and rivers — associating distance with the river — but look at you, you're like the Little Savior of the World, and Wilber Eduardo patted the boy's head, his curly hair, Rogelio and the orange T-shirt staring back at him, and José Matías thanking them, taking Mama Lola by the hand, a gentle squeeze of her callused palm to say goodbye, the Flores brothers nodding their heads, it's been a pleasure, your generosity is the sweet breath of angels, soothing the terrified soul, a truly poetic José Matías, finely turned words, Wilber Eduardo shook his head in disbelief and pleasure, and they waved to the mother and child before climbing into the pickup.

Traveling the unpaved road with the conviction of their souls — in the words of Monsignor Romero, the people's most sacred right is the right to enter a church and worship

God with the conviction of their souls — so it was their sacred right to travel that unpaved road on a journey to purify themselves, a liberation from ghosts and the past, and now it was taking them to Graciela Menéndez's parents' house, they were heading northwest once again to connect with the road that leads to Lajas y Canoas, and then to San Ildefonso, waving goodbye to Embalse 15 de Septiembre, a reservoir touched by more than a couple of rivers, moving further away from the lucid Lempa, an articulate river, speaking fluently to them, encouraging them, *¡Ustedes pueden hacerlo!* you can do it! a river that squinted blindly in the bright afternoon light.

The Flores brothers, living in fear, confusion and uncertainty, accustomed to seeing corpses — how much they needed a word of serenity, of infinite reach — and the *cadejos,* knowing this, stood firmly as was their duty, they wouldn't leave the Flores brothers no matter what — so from the world of waking dreams, where words refused to cooperate, José Matías and Wilber Eduardo, together, became passengers on a parallel journey, a little voyage elsewhere, an established reference point — in simple terms, they wanted a minor entertainment or diversion, and what follows is a bit of rest and relaxation for them while they're on the road, a diversion from all they were ruminating on, life and death — José Matías and Wilber Eduardo, on a brief excursion, for the time being, clickety-clack, on a sort of train journey in their minds' eye, clackety-click, giving in to their imagination, riding in the cab of the pickup, while heading northwest, their eyes open to watch the road, oncoming traffic — almost none — but there were other things to see, large and average-sized birds flying low on the distant horizon, a deserted village of whitewashed tumbledown houses, rolling farmland, and a Black-headed Trogon soaring into the air from the branch of a tree, following high above them for a short distance, difficult to get to, if not impossible, while time marched on, on Wilber Eduardo's watch, a gift from Gustavo, it's the best imitation you can buy, time itself marking their limitless imaginations, two minds combined, a couple of brothers riding side by side in a pickup, shared inventiveness in order to illumine their lives — in simple terms, what followed was a distraction for them, a history lesson, too, on the road, a distraction from all that they were ruminating on — what limits could their imaginations possibly know? they'd lived through and survived the two extremes of faith, all that their parents and the church had given them, and then none, a void, slamming into a believer's brick wall, their faith torn from their hearts by soldiers and guardsmen, human beings, true enough, but human beings smeared with a madness like shit that became savagery.

A DIVERTISSEMENT

Anastasio Mártir Aquino, *Rey de los Nonualcos,* a symbol of liberation against tyranny, wearing his crown of gold and emeralds taken from a statue of St Joseph in the church of *Nuestra Señora del Pilar,* he proclaimed himself king of a sovereign Indian state, it wouldn't last long but he was King of the Nonualcos, an indigenous tribe of the Pipil, and the Flores brothers, riding in the pickup, and at the same time, in a parallel world, sitting at a table with Anastasio Mártir Aquino, *Rey de los Nonualcos,* the most widely celebrated chief of the Pipils after Tutecotzinu, José Matías and Wilber Eduardo in the company of a king, Anastasio Aquino, who'd once worked on an indigo plantation in Santiago Nonualco, the three of them sitting at a table drinking *Tic tac,* an *aguardiente* just like the drinks he'd banned in mid-February 1883 in Tepetitán, a municipality in the department of San Vicente, but that was long ago, and now they were drinking and getting red in the face and the heat and the rays of the sun were pouring over them like molten lava, take from the rich and give to the poor, that's my motto, and Anastasio Aquino, laughing at his own joke, the Flores brothers, laughing with him, but in your case, *compañeros,* it's revenge and destruction pure and simple, you've got to deal with what frightened you or it'll never go away, haunted the rest of your lives — count one two three four and you're dead before you've lived — and I know you don't want that, *mis amigos.*

The music played from a pair of loudspeakers, "Perdida" by Los Panchos, Alfredo Gil and Chucho Navarro from Mexico, Hernándo Avilés from Puerto Rico, and the Flores brothers, remembering an uncle, Leoncio, who'd seen them in '51, on a tour in Latin America, their father's brother, Leoncio, nicknamed Leonc, the Flores brothers, telling their father, as if he didn't know his own brother, working every night as a musician in a dance hall, *nuestro tío no trabaja ni mucho, ni poco,* a joke because he worked all the time, but only at night, and now, hearing a song that incites to a permanent trance, a wonderful wonder, playing softly but still very present in the warm air around them, another dream or was the music really playing through loudspeakers attached to the whitewashed walls of the house they were visiting? it was music to soothe their souls, a dozen Sweet-Scented Lycaste, smelling of cinnamon, a fistful of *loroco* before cooking, a few large funnel-shaped purple flowers with yellow eyes fading to white from the maquilishuat tree, *Tabebuia rosea,* all blossoming from their ears with the music, José Matías and Wilber Eduardo, drinking *aguardiente* in the company of a king, and Anastasio Aquino himself, listening to Los Panchos sing a mournful song.

Perdida, te ha llamado la gente, sin saber que has sufrido,
con desesperación.
Vencida, quedaste tú en la vida, por no tener cariño,
que te diera ilusión.
Perdida, porque al fango rodaste, después que destrozaron,
tu virtud y tu honor.
No importa, que te llamen perdida, yo le daré a tu vida,
que destrozó el engaño, la verdad de mi amor.

Perdida, te ha llamado la gente, sin saber que has sufrido,
con desesperación.
Vencida, quedaste tú en la vida, por no tener cariño,
que te diera ilusión.
Perdida, porque al fango rodaste, después que destrozaron,
tu virtud y tu honor.
No importa, que te llamen perdida, yo le daré a tu vida,
que destrozó el engaño, la verdad de mi amor.

And when the song finished and another took its place, Anastasio Aquino, sitting up in his chair, not slumped there anymore drinking *aguardiente,* a *guaro,* I know you don't want that, *mis amigos,* repeating what he'd already said, but what I mean is books stay and people leave, that includes all of us, but José Matías, a stern expression on his face, how does that explain that you're here? you were executed, it's enough to excite the imagination, even if the legend says you charged Major Cuellar shouting, *¡Treinta arriba, treinta abajo, y adentro Santiagueños!*—which I believe, my King, representing countless myths—but you were killed by firing squad, your head cut off and shown to the world of San Vicente, it just doesn't add up with your theory that books stay and people leave, because you haven't gone anywhere, take a look at yourself! and he turned to his brother, to Wilber Eduardo, who had to agree, nodding, swallowing another mouthful, his throat burning with a taste of *Tic tac,* and the alcohol made him shiver and smile.

I'm where I want to be now that I'm dead, Anastasio Aquino, rubbing his hands together, taking a moment to look at the sky, clear of clouds, a deep blue, and a bright sun smiling down on them, I can relax now, my work is done, the villages of Santiago and San Juan Nonualco, as well as Analco and a part of the town of Zacatecoluca along with their local authorities, answered my call, accompanied by other villages around the capital, and towards the end of January—it was long ago—I could count on an army of 3000 mostly indigenous men, "my valiant lads and army comrades," so as you can see, I'm between this and that, here and there, neither ghost nor flesh and blood, but well placed to give you advice, *mis amigos* — you don't have to assemble men, you have a smaller but equally important task to carry out, for yourselves, for people who suffered as you did, and you can bring it off once you've got the talisman in your hands.

The Flores brothers, given a nudge forward by his words, each breaking into a broad smile, it wasn't the alcohol, but it helped them relax, a lubrication, and they nodded at each other with enthusiasm, a dual life, riding together in the cab of the pickup, and at the same time here with Anastasio Aquino who, continuing without boasting, gave them a little history lesson, what I mean is, if lives could be lived again, because I was an important man, what I mean is that I had extraordinary organizational skills, there was so much to do, what I mean is that I knew how to organize, my valiant lads and army comrades, what I mean is I was filled with reckless audacity, acute attention, not missing a trick, what I mean is I organized with reckless audacity — a man of amazing courage, that's what they said — Anastasio Aquino, embarrassed, but confident, giggling quietly, and smiling, too, saying in a whisper that he'd never known any fear and that he'd never been afraid of anything or anyone, and what I mean is that this distinctive characteristic assured the victory of my skillful strategies, José Matías and Wilber Eduardo, always willing to learn, they were ignoring their drinks, gripping the arms of their respective chairs, and Anastasio Aquino, I count my blessings to be in the same company as Túpac Amaru, the last indigenous Inca monarch, who after the death of his brothers, succeeding to the title *Sapa Inca,* in Vilcabamba, fought the Spanish conquerors, but it's a long story, and a sad one, not unlike my own, *mis amigos,* and we aren't here to tell all the tales there are to tell in the whole of the world.

José Matías and Wilber Eduardo, wanting to join in, to tell Anastasio Aquino what they knew of his life, only a little bit, not more than that, out of respect, taking turns recounting the story, one and the same voice coming from each brother, and yet no words, it was a parallel life, one in the pickup and the other in a sort of dream, the Flores brothers, you refused to join the army the government of Mariano Prado set up for civil wars for which many villagers were recruited, the most affected villages, San Juan and Santiago Nonualco, each losing members of their tribes, and so you said: "Let's retaliate together and not obey the government of El Salvador, let's deny them the right to recruit people and impose taxes on us like they've been doing for so long, oppressing us, sending us to die far away from our families, let's fight to the death for our cause and I'll be your general."

And then, the Flores brothers, José Matías and Wilber Eduardo, still leaning forward in their chairs, their two cents became a dollar, showing off a bit, Anastasio Mártir Aquino, *Rey de los Nonualcos,* your brother tethered like an animal to a *trozo,* a piece of wood, by the owner of the hacienda, it was too much to bear, my King, and the brutality—the unendurable way your fellow villagers were recruited for the army—and personal tax, tributes and expropriations, life was becoming impossible, life as it is was impossible, my King, so you organized an uprising with twenty-five men, the first insurrectional act of laborers whose land was taken by the aristocracy, catching the soldiers of Zacatecoluca, the capital municipality of the department of La Paz, in the Río Lempa valley at the foot of Chinchontepec, *Las Chiches,* catching the soldiers unprepared, defeating them, returning to Santiago Nonualco with weapons, new men joining your forces along the way, and later, defeating the official troops sent to San Salvador to conquer the Nonualcos, it was the battle of *Las Vueltas del Loco* — the going mad — and in the battle, calculating the exact moment they'd be passing, positioning your soldiers to surprise them before they could act, and when they appeared, you confronted the enemy, shouting: "Arms or life!" and "Go on, you valiant villagers of Santiago!" and other warrior's words, but finally — a great task comes to an end — after this battle, the government soldiers in Consejo, preparing a trap for you, the unlucky one — we can only say you were unlucky — a traitor delivered you to the government, *Rey de los Nonualcos,* my King, and you were caught in Tacuazín, like the word for the opossum, Tacuazín, god of the dawn, and executed in San Vicente — Anastasio Mártir Aquino, an exemplary fighter, the commander of the uprising.

Anastasio Aquino, *Rey de los Nonualcos,* a skin infection from an old wound on his arm appearing out of nowhere, or embarrassment, out of nervousness, too many glorious compliments from the Flores brothers for his own good, and José Matías, feeling responsible, remembering a tincture made from the bark of the *marañón,* the cashew tree, he reached into a satchel and took a brown glass bottle out of a small pocket, the bottle contained the tincture from the bark of the *marañón* that could be applied to the skin, handing the bottle to Anastasio Aquino, here, take this, my King, and Anastasio Aquino, smiling, nodding his head, you do it, *curandero,* I can't reach it properly, and José Matías, I'm not a healer, but I'll do it just the same, with pleasure, and Wilber Eduardo, leaning back in his chair, stretching his arms above his head, the *Tic tac* made him sleepy, and the talk, they'd been speaking for hours sitting there under the sun, and Wilber Eduardo, herpes explodes on my lip if I get too hot in the burning sun, a sun like this one, a few words to ease the self-consciousness he thought the King might've felt, or there was no embarrassment because it was an old wound, there was a definite expression of pride, a deep wound from battle in the skin of a warrior's arm, but then Wilber Eduardo shut his mouth, he'd said enough, and Anastasio Aquino, looking up at the sun without a pair of sunglasses while José Matías applied the tincture to the infection on his arm.

In seconds the infection disappeared, it wasn't the tincture, José Matías was sure of it, but a sort of magic, something that came from the contact of the tincture of bark of the *marañón* with Anastasio Mártir Aquino's skin, *Rey de los Nonualcos* — a thirst for political justice, a pride in his Indian heritage, and a huge ego — Wilber Eduardo yawning, covering his mouth quickly with his hand, this is no time to show disrespect, he was falling asleep in the cab of the pickup at the same time as he was sitting with his brother and Anastasio Aquino, drowsiness must've crept over the line, from one realm to the other, the dual life, and Wilber Eduardo, a traveler who passed between different times, I'm counting on it to carry me all the way to Graciela Menéndez's parents' house, and beyond, a way to keep my mind off things, riding with his brother in the cab of the pickup and here, at the same time, with the immeasurably popular Anastasio Aquino, a symbol of rebellion and symbol of symbols, and like a persistent rain, the slow surprise of a memory flooded with memories, a grip of the all mighty you-better-let-me-go-or-I'll-scream that wouldn't release them, the Flores brothers, they felt the grip, holding them, keeping them alive and living in the ever-so-important parallel world on a parallel journey, a brotherly and shared dream that kept them afloat in flight from some ghost or monster in a Mexican horror movie, maybe *El barón del terror.*

A step off the train carrying Anastasio Mártir Aquino, José Matías and Wilber Eduardo, a couple of chips off the old block and a friendly ghost, *Rey de los Nonualcos*, from Santiago Nonualco, wise as wise can be — not really a train with a locomotive but a train of thought — leaving a compartment of their imagination made for distraction and a broadening of the mind, serving the purpose of drawing the Flores brothers out of fear of what they'd seen, maybe a ghost or monster in a Mexican horror movie, José Matías and Wilber Eduardo and the *cadejos*, together, traveling in a pickup to San Ildefonso, leaving behind the table and chairs in the burning sun, leaving behind drinking *Tic tac,* leaving behind the whole encounter with Anastasio Mártir Aquino — a blend, a union, and a concoction of age and experience — a man from two centuries back, and the other two, the Flores brothers, of the twentieth century, born two years apart, and brothers in all things, especially a colossal and terrifying suffering at the hands of the *Guardia Nacional,* and at the hands of the *Policía Nacional,* or the hands of the *Policía de Hacienda,* and plenty of soldiers' hands, torture and horror, José Matías and Wilber Eduardo, brothers of experience, and memory, too, victims of *El honor es nuestra divisa,* a motto of the *Guardia Nacional,* so impossible to believe even then, the Flores brothers stepped off the imaginary train — how long they were sitting in the sun with Anastasio Aquino, they didn't know, for no watch in the world kept that sort of time, a time out of step with any form of measurement — leaving Anastasio Aquino, King of the Nonualcos, an indigenous tribe of the Pipil, drinking *Tic tac,* an *aguardiente,* behind them, while all the time riding, in fact, in the cab of the pickup — how many places could they be in at once? — the Flores brothers, finding themselves back in the cab of the pickup, changing scenes, in order to follow the story Graciela Menéndez had told them of the talisman buried in the backyard of her parents' house, a story she told them not long ago.

Tears grooving Graciela's face, she couldn't help it, a memory pressing down on her tear ducts, a couple of words reminding her of her own fears, it wasn't that long ago, you can count the years, and Graciela wiping the tears away with a moisturized hand, skin as smooth as silk, the Flores brothers repeating, we're screwed, we think we're really screwed, and we can't shake it off, José Matías and Wilber Eduardo, almost whispering, confiding in Graciela Menéndez, and Concepción, smoking a cigarillo, listening to everything everyone said, ears like a jaguar, and a cloud of smoke in Gustavo's face, coughing, spilling a little beer, Concepción, what now boys? do you think it's as bad as all that? think about it and then you'll come to the same conclusion I came to when I gave it a couple of minutes and decided that there's nothing, here and now, to compare, not really, with how things used to be, and they're not going to get worse but better, my conviction, cross my heart, and Emiliano, so you're an optimist, no laughing, Graciela Menéndez's arms covered in lotion, glistening in the sunlight, smooth and soft to the touch, the Flores brothers watching the grace of Graciela, but they wouldn't dare put a hand on her, it wasn't how José Matías and Wilber Eduardo lived, not after what they'd been through, although she was just as good looking as she'd ever been, nothing seemed to put an ounce of weight on her, there wasn't a wrinkle on her skin, maybe a few lines near a pair of eyes that smiled — as I live and breathe, *mis amigos,* ha! what a sense of humor! — no matter what happened, and no matter how desperate life became, Graciela Menéndez, always finding a way to toss a laugh up in the air for anyone and everyone to catch on its way down.

The only thing that matters is to work and get on with our lives, Concepción, taking a lungful of smoke and sending it out in Gustavo's direction, Gustavo ducking like she'd thrown a punch, grinning, you're a real philosopher, Concha, Gustavo getting back at her on account of the smoke, spilling his beer, not all of it, just a little, but every drop counts, and Emiliano, having finished his lunch, another day and another *pupusa revuelta*, pork, beans, loroco, today no cheese, spicy tomato salsa and *curtido* on the side, picking his teeth to remove bits of beans and pork, and Emiliano, the majority consensus of our people — Gustavo interrupting him, don't start on that Leo, we're up to our ears in your politics, and where did it get you, remember Los Llanitos in Cabañas, when you stuck your neck out in '84? no wonder Lucía stayed at home, and Emiliano, looking at Benavides for support, Benavides paying attention to no one and nothing but the birds circling overhead, Emiliano saying, what do you make of it, Benavides? but Benavides rolling his eyes, and Concepción, pointing at Emiliano, hang on, El Puño, she always called him the Fist, everyone else called him Leo, don't drag him into it, he's got nothing to say about anything but the birds and the bees, it was a sweet joke for Concepción, because Benavides, fucked up by the soldiers of the National Guard, the murder of three hundred farmers on the banks of Río Sumpul in Chalatenango, and she reached out past Gustavo to tickle Benavides, a little simpleminded, on account of being beaten, Benavides, who tipped over on his side into the grass, laughing and singing her praises.

Graciela Menéndez, leaning to her right, her elbow in the grass, whispering to José Matías and Wilber Eduardo, not wanting the others to hear, asking the Flores brothers, what is it? what's on your mind? and they answered in one voice, "the wind caught up with us, the trees bent until they creaked and tossed their branches in desperation," you know how it goes, Clara Isabel Alegría Vides, words strung together by a wizard, and Graciela Menéndez, moved by their voices, and the voice of a poet, in a firm, husky voice of her own, scratch the surface and there's the world, *mis amigos,* and the Flores brothers, not poker-faced but grim, insisting, we felt the danger like a slicing wind, it's around the corner, or straight ahead, but we don't know when or where it'll strike, like lightning, so put yourself in our place, Graciela, we're facing an unpleasant climate.

Concepción, Emiliano, Gustavo and Benavides, eight eyes fixed all at once on the Flores brothers and Graciela Menéndez, who were getting up from where they were sitting on the ground, relaxing in a park, a slow easy walking forward, a stand of tall slender shade trees, turning away from them, heading toward the sun, or a single large tree, not as tall or slender, with full overhanging branches, maybe a mango, and at last coming to a massive ceiba tree, which for the Maya connected the planes of the underworld, *Xibalbá,* and the terrestrial realm and the skies, *Xibalbá* where souls of the dead, "if they had been of good conduct, entered a place where nothing would give pain, where there would be an abundance of food and delicious drinks, and a refreshing and shady tree they called *Yaxché,* the ceiba tree, beneath whose branches and shade they might rest and be in peace forever," according to Friar Diego de Landa, *Relación de las Cosas de Yucatán,* and the Flores brothers, and Graciela Menéndez, a silk-cotton tree, the ceiba, would soon protect them from the sun, and, a few yards away from the others, they sat down again, beneath the *Yaxché,* the ceiba tree, out of ear shot, with their backs leaning against the thorny trunk of the tree, it's leafy branches swaying in a wind that caressed the faces of all who lay before it.

THE STORY OF THE TALISMAN

Graciela Menéndez, whispering at first, then realizing it was a waste of energy, she didn't have to, the wind blew in a direction away from the others, to her advantage, and they were sitting far enough from Concepción, Emiliano, Gustavo and Benavides to keep what she had to say a secret from them, suspicion still ran in her veins, whether she liked it or not, so Graciela Menéndez, a deep breath, I remember something Monsignor Romero said, maybe it was in a book by Bencastro, magnificent, did you ever read it? anyway, it was something Monsignor Romero said about a strike by the Mass Revolutionary Coordinating Committee, a protest against repression, an attempt to denounce a situation that was intolerable, like your own, *mis amigos,* my Flores brothers, like all our situations, in the past, and I want to help you, I want to offer you something which will take away the fear behind the words you spoke to me, "We're really screwed," it must be something serious or you wouldn't have said it, those words you confided in me — brothers of a wounded generation, just as I am your sister, a grown woman and survivor, like you, victims of violence — and like the Monsignor said, it wasn't just a protest, a denunciation, it was also political, demonstrating that repression, instead of intimidating the popular organizations, it was fortifying them, which is the point I'm trying to make, you have to show whatever it is that's making you feel like you're screwed that you're strong, that no matter what it does to you, you aren't going to buckle under the titanic stress, just like the earth, shift and shift, you see what I mean? and in his exact words, "Here we think of the dead, victims of cruelty, and of those who continue to live, but in terror, under threat, bearing in their bodies the marks of torture, of outrages committed against them," so show them what you're made of — a cliché, I know, but there you go — words are words as long as we use them for a good cause, I'm the biggest believer in mysteries — and with strength comes resolve, action and change.

And the Flores brothers, in one voice, we didn't mean anything specific because we don't know what it is, not yet, but a dread, an anvil's weight, something hanging over us, over our heads, that we can't describe but feel just the same, like a premonition, a creeping suspicion that's more like a hunch that it'll be one-fine-day-and-bang! right between the eyes! and that's what we're afraid of, we're afraid it's going to kill us, and what you've got to say, and the Monsignor, together, his words and yours, and you, willing to help us, a lifelong friend, your beautiful skin, glistening in the shade of this ceiba, a silk-cotton tree, your skin, smooth and soft to the touch, but we wouldn't dare, really, though it's crossed our minds — you've always been a favorite, Wilber Eduardo admitted, blushing — it'll be enough if you can give us some advice.

Nobody wants to surprise Death standing there, with no sense of humor, half expecting us, arms folded and waiting patiently, Graciela Menéndez, dropping her gaze from the sky to the ground, biting her lip while thinking about what she'd said, then asking José Matías for a smoke, he took the pack from his shirt pocket, knocked a cigarette out and shoved the pack under her slender nose, not as wide as her little brother's nose, graceful Graciela Menéndez, her hands steady as they took the cigarette, and Wilber Eduardo, I didn't know you smoked, Graciela Menéndez, I don't, but the smoke from your stinking cigarettes will keep the bad spirits away, I don't want anybody listening to what I have to say, and to Wilber Eduardo, you take one, too, and José Matías, smoke one yourself, let's all have one, you enjoy it so why keep from smoking on my account now that we're getting down to fundamentals, straight from the horse's mouth, ha! maybe you know the movie? let's light up! my Flores brothers, and José Matías and Wilber Eduardo, their heads turning at the same time with the same speed, giving Graciela Menéndez the eye, giving her all four of them, it wasn't what they were expecting to come out of her mouth, and the Flores brothers, holding back a laugh, but it didn't last, they started giggling self-consciously.

At noon, the white clouds, swollen large, floating low over the houses, nestling close to the town, and Graciela Menéndez, a pause, her story hadn't really begun, but it was a poetic beginning, Graciela Menéndez, blowing cigarette smoke to the left and right, don't be so lazy, Wilber Eduardo, make like a smokestack, and if you have to cough, then cough, Graciela Menéndez giving them a smile, her perfect teeth, not like her brother's teeth, starting her story again, roosters crow at all hours of the day or night, and here we are leaning against this tree, a ceiba whose branches are themselves horizontal trees, ancient, its roots traveling into the earth, *Xibalbá* — remember where we are, where we've been, where we'll go, *mis amigos* — and shading us from sunlight, a perfect place to tell you the story of the talisman, if you don't already know it, and the Flores brothers, together, with one gesture and shaking their heads to say no, they hadn't heard her tell the story of the talisman, we want to know, Graciela Menéndez, we really want to know and you must tell us, and Wilber Eduardo blew a cloud of smoke out in front of him, showing his conviction in her methods, a solidarity with her magic, his brother smoking leisurely, the wind at once still and warm, caressing their faces, while the others, Concepción, Emiliano, Gustavo and Benavides — Lucía was at work, Margó was in school, Alfonso was teaching — they were cleaning up the mess they'd made, it was a public park, a picnic, bottles of Pilsener and Suprema, orange soda and Coca-Cola in plastic bags with straws, *soda en bolsa*, a thermos empty of weak black coffee with sugar, ceramic cups from Graciela's kitchen, a box for Concepción's handmade cigars, an almost empty container of homemade sweet, pineapple *Semita* cakes, a greasy bag with nothing left of Emiliano's *pupusas revueltas* with pork and beans and loroco, a tomato salsa of hot chile peppers and onion, no cheese, spicy tomato salsa and *curtido* on the side, he'd learned his lesson — not like the last time at Margó's birthday, although the past is part of the future, Lucía was there, Margó clapping her hands, and Alfonso, a day he wasn't teaching — but now was today, a picnic in the park, the wind suddenly blowing a gust containing a few of Concepción's words in their direction, Graciela Menéndez, José Matías and Wilber Eduardo, turning their heads, hearing Concha's words, don't forget to gather up the dirty plates and paper napkins, El Puño, before the wind really picks up and blows them all over the place.

Our Savior of the Flores Brothers, she didn't lose her place, a memory as sharp as a snapping turtle's jaws, once she's got a hold on something, lookout! Graciela Menéndez, continuing her story, it was around noon, that's what I was saying, when the white clouds swelled large and floated low over the houses, snuggling up to the sleeping town — you must have read it somewhere — the clouds changing from white to gray with each step I took on the unpaved road — it was suddenly so dark for that time of day — and a light in a window drawing attention away from my thoughts, thoughts wandering a bit here, a bit there, but formed in every way by the death of my little brother, ruminating on the nature of existence, or in his case, nonexistence, since Segundo was dead, after all, and there was nothing anyone, especially me, could do to bring him back, and José Matías and Wilber Eduardo, each releasing a cloud of cigarette smoke, I thought your brother's name was Nelson, and Graciela Menéndez, offering another blinding smile, a knockout, exhaling smoke through her nose, yes, but he was the second born, I always called him Segundo, even though his was named Nelson, *mis amigos,* my Flores brothers, but let me continue, so I went toward the house that wasn't more than a shack, a kind of *jacal,* like in Mexico, but poverty, that's all, an iguana tied with a string to a stake near the front door, a sturdy shack but not as bad as all that, not as bad as you imagine — I see it in your eyes, all four of them, feeling sorry for the climate of the place — but don't be deceived, because someone lived in that house, and I've always believed and believe to this day that where a person lives, that place is always a home, no matter what it looks like, inside or out, and where the light shone in a window, I walked cautiously toward it, it was a beacon of hope, a sign for me that I must approach, inescapably drawn to the house, to come near to what I didn't know but maybe feared, yet the light I saw sent out warmth to sooth the chill in my heart while dwelling on the death of Segundo, and I wasn't afraid.

The light of the sky fell to the earth, like a switch had been hit, as soon as I stepped onto the tiny porch, so I stopped for a second just in front of the door of the little house, a house that gave me the impression it'd been abandoned for years, but the light in the window couldn't have been lit by a ghost, as far as I know, ghosts don't have our fingers or toes, and the door was ajar and there was humming, under breath — ok, it wasn't me — of a living, breathing human being that came from the other side of the wall, the one facing the unpaved road, and hearing that humming, a kind of innocence, brought my worries into the light, so to speak — as it was almost dark at the hour of one o'clock in the afternoon — and I wasn't afraid anymore, or at least I wasn't so frozen with fear that I couldn't fulfill a promise to my curiosity.

The white clouds, large and floating low over the houses, had changed from white to gray and now threatened rain, full and heavy clouds ready to burst at the seams just above my head — you could taste the moisture in the air, *mis amigos* — and less to get out of the inevitable storm, more from inquisitiveness, I stuck out my foot and let the toe of my shoe push the door just a little bit, in order to prove to myself it was truly ajar, and I decided at once to go in after knocking, I'd waited for a reply from within which didn't come, and then, gathering the courage that coursed through my muscles and nerves, I stepped over the threshold.

My nose, which you never cease to compliment, as unlike my brother's nose as a nose could be, may Segundo rest in eternal peace, was as active as Ilamatepec — a dominantly andesitic to trachyandesitic stratovolcano rising immediately west of Coatepeque caldera, *Lago de Coatepeque*, just in case you forgot your school studies, my Flores brothers, whose broad summit is cut by several crescentic craters, and a long series of parasitic vents and cones that formed along a twenty-kilometer-long fissure system extending from near the town of Chalchuapa, north-northwest of the volcano, to the San Marcelino and Cerro la Olla cinder cones on the southeast flank — and the odors that impregnated the floor and walls of the shack, a kind of *jacal*, jumped at my nose, precious as a gem, you might say, making me take a step backward, then two steps forward into the edge of a wooden table I didn't see on account of a single kerosene lamp in the window whose flame was blocked out by a photograph that leaned against it.

I bent over, folded like a sheet of paper, flexible as I was then, not stiff and achy as I am now, and rubbed my bruised thigh, it was a bruise just above the knee, wanting to kick the table out of my way, a temper as always, but it wasn't my table and it wasn't my house, so I looked up to see what I could see of the room — I didn't get a good look at the photograph until later — making out of the shadows a flat rectangular shape of glass in a frame, propped against the lamp, reflecting a little of what was in front of it, and from where I was standing, the glass a blank for the most part, when suddenly the room was lit by a lightning bolt shooting out of the sky as it started to rain, and there was a woman sitting in a threadbare low-standing chair, facing the kerosene lamp and the window from which I'd seen the light burning.

My life stood still at this moment, while nature and man-made things took over: a plane flying over the dark, damp house, passing through the rapidly darkening sky, the noise of its engines increasing then fading, the woman sitting in the chair, it wasn't a cane rocking chair but it creaked when she moved, turning her head toward me — I saw her from what seemed like far away — and the sound of thunder following lightning, the air maybe fifty thousand degrees, I couldn't measure it, but rapidly expanding, vibrating the air, a shock wave expanding away from the lightning stroke — when you see lightning and then hear thunder soon after, you should always go inside a sturdy building until it's safe to return outside — and the woman, what are you looking at? show a little respect for the dead, you aren't scared are you? breaking the spell, staring at me as I stared at her, the force of her stare, an ache in my heart, a hand to my chest, I felt my heart beating, I'm not — interrupting myself, my voice was whispering, I'm not scared of any-thing, but yes, I'm looking at you, I guess, and the woman, yes, *m'hija,* you're looking at me.

And of course she was right, my Flores brothers, where was I supposed to look? and at the same time, I was waiting for the plane's next sweep, but nothing, it must've gone on its way or the sound of the engine was lost in peals of thunder, the rain started to pour, lashing against the window, but inside the shack, a kind of *jacal,* but nothing like it, it was someone's home and wasn't a shack or rundown place — dignity, we've all got our dignity, *mis amigos* — inside the shack it was dry and safe from rain and lightning, and gradually the rain settled to a steady drumming, a concert of sounds, a leaden curtain enveloping the trees and streets and houses and shacks like *jacales,* if you want to call them that, but I hesitate, really, to say anything but good about them, Sergio Ramírez coming to mind, his descriptions, but let's get back to my own story, and the talisman, *mis amigos,* brothers, my Flores brothers.

So immediately, the woman, what a voice she had, a strength in it I can't describe, not like thunder, what can I say? commanding and self-confident, nothing ethereal about this ghost, if she really was a ghost — I didn't have any experience with ghosts — and there were snatches of conversation, I swear I heard voices, but they weren't loud enough to understand, a sort of background noise made of voices, and the woman started speaking, you might as well know my name on account of you've come into my house uninvited, it's Blanca, *m'hija,* and I can grow a tree right here in front of you, the woman getting up from her chair, the chair creaking, crossing the room to the bed she slept in — if she slept at all, I don't know anything about such things — reaching under it, dragging a heavy-looking trunk out from beneath the bed without scraping the floor, a weight she handled like it was a trunk made of balsa and filled with feathers, then reaching in the open trunk, a lot of noise, clanging and banging like pots and pans as she was digging around, accompanied by the faraway voices I couldn't understand—I didn't know what she was looking for, but she was looking like fury for something—turning her head toward me, how about a *tihuilote* tree, *jovencita*? and I'll make it come right out of the floor, you'll like that, won't you? it'll be the first time, something new, and a story to tell your children, a strange choked laughter came out of her throat like bottles rattling as crates were stacked, then a vigorous sigh, the wind, and relief, quiet, she held a very old book in her hand, a couple of loose papers, too, and the others, in the book, tied neatly together, bound in a worn green cardboard binding, or the covers were made of dark green linen, water-stained, and worn out from fingers riffling through the pages.

Blinking into the gloom, the kerosene lamp didn't light up very much of the room, I was speechless, and the woman, Blanca, clearing her throat hesitantly, relax, *m'hija*, there's plenty of time for feeling uncomfortable in this life, you're young, so have a seat while I make the *tihuilote* tree rise out of the floor, you'll love it, really, and it'll make your eyes water real tears of joy.

I tried, in the silence that followed, to be patient—I was in a sort of trance, and then there was my inborn, constitutional curiosity—sitting in a chair she'd indicated with a bony finger, a chair I hadn't seen but found by feeling my way in the dimly lit room without banging into anything, *mis amigos,* scraping the soles of my shoes on the floor, not lifting a foot to move forward, taking an indecisive stride, then another, afraid to step on something, to break something, or crush a cat's tail, for example, because, who knows what's in Blanca's place, living or dead. My eyes were open, watching what I couldn't see clearly, but right away, prayers and incense, a bundle of dried plants she'd taken out of a drawer in the table I hit with my leg, a bruise above the knee, Blanca lighting the incense with wooden matches, a heavy cloud of smoke quickly filling the room, the rain, a steady drumming, and the faraway voices, gossiping and prattling on, a concert of sounds, I couldn't understand a word of what they were saying, and here, in this part of the world, electricity was still dim, meals were cooked on wood fires, dogs still barked and roosters crowed through the night, the thunderbolts crashed to earth, shaking volcanoes to their foundations.

And if you said there must've been a lot of wondering jumping around in your head, my sweet Graciela Menéndez, our wonderful wonder of an angel Graciela Menéndez, you'd be right, it was nothing short of that, a swirl of asking asked by a confused but thoroughly interested observer and voluntary captive of the baffling Blanca, eyes shut tight, standing in front of me with her incense and her prayers, and god knows what else I'd go through in the minutes or hours to come — what do you see? a lack of anything clear is what you see, what's going on? Blanca and the business of the *tihuilote* tree is what's going on — and words are words, but she was praying a storm full, a roomful of words, Blanca the ghost or Blanca the witch, and the rain started to pour again, lashing against the window, each drop of rain hit the roof with a distinct sound, a pleasing resting place, a distinct sound of one-inch glass marbles falling from heaven.

What happened next is still what was happening to me, because she stopped praying and looked at me through a cloud of incense that smelled of earth, redolent of all things that grow, like flowers and trees and plants and grass, and even the smell of dirt itself, *mis amigos,* I could smell that too, and Blanca, a gaze as straight as an arrow aimed at my forehead, Blanca saying, I do *not* fall into a trance, I have supernatural vision, the incense and prayers are for cleansing, and with nothing to say in reply, nodding my head, as agreeable as someone who's bewitched can be, an accomplice, really, to what was passing before my eyes, and it was only the beginning, I knew it then as I tell it now, and Blanca, a woman or man can travel beyond the borders of a country, you can't deny it, whether in this life or the next, visiting other places — knowledge and skills, skills and knowledge — and as long as we aren't ghosts locked into the place of our living body's death, an ordinary woman or man, living or dead, they can travel, and she switched on the radio standing in a corner of the room, it was playing *rancheras,* and Blanca, there's truly magic in all living beings, even the radio, *m'hija,* and she was back to the heavy-looking trunk, reaching in, her arms disappearing up to her elbows, and a lot of noise, more clanging and banging like pots and pans.

The music didn't shut out the noise of the rain falling like marbles on the roof, and Blanca, looking sad, for a ghost or a witch, a witch or a ghost, I couldn't say what she was, but there was something like sorrow crowding in on her face — someone should've given her body three turns to the right and four to the left, seven in all, to confuse the soul so that it couldn't return to this life of misery — Blanca, standing up, I couldn't see what she'd taken out of the trunk, and she was talking to herself, then there's the soul, and companion animal spirits, in harmony with our personality, with the strength of our souls, and these animal spirits, wild animals, jaguars, foxes, deer, anteaters, weasels, owls, hawks — the true identity of a person's companion animal spirit is revealed in dreams, no question why men dream, they dream to live a full life, and they dream to save their lives, and Blanca, looking past me at the rain falling against the window, past the kerosene lamp, but that's not what I want to say to you now, it's another story, *m'hija,* because I want to show you something else, you're here to see the *tihuilote* tree rise out of the floor, isn't that right? so for the moment, patience, and relax, have confidence in miraculous events, and she looked away from the window, and my startled face staring back at her without a word in my mouth, but how could I relax, *mis amigos,* when I was puzzled by what awaited me? and then Blanca, all at once she was very tall, Blanca casting a long shadow grown out of I don't know which light shining on her, because there was only the kerosene lamp, and now and then a bolt of lightning from a sky throwing rain down to the earth in handfuls.

Her shadow was a frightening shadow as it stretched the length of the shack — a kind of *jacal,* but nothing like it, you can believe me — and watching the shadow, its arms and legs wavering like a flame in candlelight without a single candle in sight and the only flame in the room behind the glass of a kerosene lamp, but her head and arms and legs wavering just the same, I looked up from the shadow and Blanca was transformed, I'm sure of it, into a form I couldn't identify—like it or not, deny it or not, affirm it or not, Blanca made an obscure sign with her finger on her forehead, a sort of volatile hieroglyphic, before transforming herself—and for a face, a blur like smudged ink, and I threw up in a bucket she'd put next to the chair.

Blanca, she was a sort of ectoplasm, a viscous substance, with a different voice, a resounding voice, I think about you dead over there, I couldn't bury you, a voice speaking to Blanca, speaking to itself, and an unfortunate figure in front of me, heart-rending, I felt a kind of tightness in my chest, the radio standing in a corner of the room was still playing music, Antonio Aguilar—you probably know him—El Charro de México, Antonio Aguilar singing "Por el amor a mi madre," and the viscous substance exuded from Blanca's body was talking to itself, to Blanca, really, long and thin and wavering still like the flame of a candle, head almost touching the ceiling, how serious it was! but what could I really see, *mis amigos?* the ectoplasm took another form, now covered head to toe with raw unrefined sugar—calcium, potassium, magnesium, copper, and iron—crystallized with honey, sweet without being sticky, a flavor of caramel, Blanca was behind all this, she was this other almost ugly transformation, maybe flavored with orange peel, a solid block of dark sugar, something sweet, a very tall dessert, a *chancaca?* a *panela* with a head and arms and legs—a bit like a stone, not like *metate,* not made from lava—and my eyes opened wide, concentrating, looking straight at a tall dessert with a head and arms and legs, I couldn't see Blanca, not there, but I knew she was somewhere in that thing in front of me, I'd bet on it, but none of this was happening, I told myself, shivering the cold of the dead and wanting to vomit again, a lump in my throat, a violent Adam's apple, rising and falling, giving me plenty of trouble, leaping, no frog hiding there, I told myself, and swallowing, my Flores brothers, it was too much, and before I knew it I was leaning over the bucket letting go everything in my guts.

Raw, unrefined sugar crystallized with honey, flavored with orange peel, I couldn't believe it, *mis amigos,* a great big block of something sweet that made me think of the Golem, Rabbi Loew, and the ghetto of Prague — counseled from Heaven to make the Golem, Rabbi Loew, making an artificial man with the help of Kabbalistic magic, by means of mystical formulas communicated to him in dreams, it was shaped in clay, endowed with spiritual breath, and made a doer of wonders, pure love of humanity justified the creation of the dreadful, and sanctified the terrible — you know it, don't you? you've got to read it if you haven't read it, my Flores brothers, write it down when you've got a minute — and the ectoplasm, the dessert, another form of Blanca, like a solid block of dark sugar, and for a face, a blur like smudged ink, walking clumsily across the small room, stopping in front of the picture frame, the glass reflecting a light that illuminated the picture, and I saw it, I saw the photograph, it was a young woman, who might've been Blanca herself at a very young age.

The viscous substance in its special form, no longer human, if that's what it'd been, not Blanca, was saying, if I had a good book, then maybe things would be different, and I felt sorry for it, *noyollo xitinia ica tlaocoyaliztli* — my heart was breaking with sadness, if you don't know the language — and even though I couldn't get out of the chair, stuck there like I'd been glued to the seat, I wanted to help it, and I was beginning to crave something sweet, too, maybe it was nerves, but I didn't think once of taking a bite out of the very tall dessert, a *chancaca* or *panela* with a head and arms and legs, the ectoplasm in another form, and then all at once I understood that it wasn't a good book that it was wishing for but a book that would serve a purpose, I didn't see it right away, thinking at first that a supernatural viscous substance, exuded from Blanca's body, now a *panela* with a head and arms and legs, wanted to sit down to read, though with what pair of eyes I couldn't say.

The very tall dessert, the thing that wasn't the Golem or *metate*, with thick, clumsy limbs, turned away from the photograph, groping around in the semi-darkness — the flame from the kerosene lamp didn't light up the room — and as if I were dreaming, I knew right away it was looking for some coffee, and so without preparing it, just like that, now it was drinking coffee, and the block of dark sugar, the transformed ectoplasm, what might've been its fingers, stubby and sugary, were stirring the coffee, and they dissolved in the coffee as a sweetener, and the whole figure became Blanca again, tall and slender, arms and legs wavering like a flame, each limb quivering, apart from the others, to a different rhythm, she'd returned to the form of Blanca, and her fingers, grasping at nothing I could see, grasping the air itself, and out of the air she plucked a heavy book, a volume containing magic spells, and Blanca, still a resounding voice, without these words, there's no incantation to raise a *tihuilote* tree from the floor, it was Blanca again, and an almost familiar voice, a peculiar odor, a spectral breath, I was asking myself to what purpose it would serve, this *tihuilote* tree, once it'd been conjured out of the earth, out of the floor in front of me, or was it merely the ectoplasm, the tall dessert or Blanca showing off?

She opened the book, turned pages, searching, it seemed to me, for a particular formula — I prayed it wasn't a curse — and I thought of Rabbi Loew again, directing a dream-question to Heaven, receiving the answer in words in alphabetical order: Ato Bra Golem Devuk Hakhomer V'tigzar Zedim Chevel Torfe Yisroel, and Rabbi Loew, arranging these words according to formulas laid down in the Book of Creation, the Rabbi filled with conviction that he'd be able, with the help of the letters revealed to him by Heaven, to make a living body out of clay — I was frightened, wondering what spell she would find and speak, how it would affect me, praying, ceremoniously thoughtful, that it'd be her elixir of life, I didn't dare take my eyes off her, your wonderful wonder of an angel Graciela Menéndez singing and cursing half the world, but as long as she remained who or what she was everything was okay, because I didn't want to see the solid block of raw unrefined sugar crystallized with honey ever again, even if it contained the healthy ingredients of calcium, potassium, magnesium, copper, and iron. I was frozen where I sat on a chair Blanca had pointed to with a bony finger.

Maybe I was dreaming, time passed without giving me a clue, no minutes or seconds went by or it could've been a thousand seconds, a hundred minutes — dead air that I breathe as I live — and Blanca, holding the book in front of her face, a blur like smudged ink, but a face, as far as I could tell, and she wore a bird talisman, it must've been a small bird, a skull, its tiny beak — a shape that mimics instruments of weaponry, penetration and intimacy — with bird feathers, a thread around her neck, magic powers or good luck, inhabited by a spirit, an enchanted bird, symbolic of vigor, energy, sexual potency, and Blanca, speaking words I couldn't understand, it was the beginning all right, it was an incantation, a low rumbling, lightning and thunder, a whirlwind of words that were garbled, incoherent, unintelligible, but they shook the room, the entire shack, a kind of *jacal*, Blanca using coins and magic powders, and lightning striking the earth, not so far away, a bolt of lightning illuminating the room, counting one thousand one, one thousand two, one thousand three, one thousand four — every five seconds equals one mile — and thunder crashing, a demented ghost or witch twisting like a snake in the dimly-lit room, my knees bouncing up and down, out of control, my arms trembling like I'd caught a horrible disease, there's no way I'm going to live through this nightmare, I told myself, and the lightning and sound of thunder outside mingled with the booming words spoken ever louder by a madwoman, coins scattering on the floor at my feet, magic powder fluttering down as misty colored clouds — what was the matter? where was the problem? my body was sealed under a thousand and one blankets of wonder, I was pure as white parchment, without a birth certificate to certify the journey, my head outlining one, two, three circles corresponding to the three gusts of wind expelled from Blanca's mouth — I didn't know what was shaking more, my arms and legs, or the room itself from the incantation recited, taken out of the book in Blanca's hands, words conjuring I don't know what because I lost consciousness, *mis amigos,* without realizing it.

As if nothing at all had happened, nothing at all, moving straight from eternity to eternity, that's what I say, because I don't know how long I was out, but when I woke up, my head was dizzy, the wave of nausea was gone, Blanca was standing there in front of me, bent over to look into my eyes, with an imitation of a nothings-going-on-here face, a wet washcloth draped over my forehead, and her stare, a gleam of light in the center of each pupil, a luminous litany of light, repeating itself like a Biblical verse, pulsing into my head — what it was doing to my mind I didn't know — an intrusion I couldn't ward off by shaking my head to say no, so I thought of a real bender I'd finished at Chico's Bar, and other bars full of binges, because I wanted to be anywhere but where I was right now.

There wasn't a bucket of my vomit next to me, nothing to prove my discomfort under the circumstances, but I was stretched tight between two worlds like a strip of elastic, in here or out there, to stay or to leave this shack, waiting for the devouring locusts, and Blanca, reading my thoughts, the great event awaits you like an explosion, *m'hija,* it's time I show you the *tihuilote* tree, and I couldn't help myself, words pouring out of my mouth, what was that all about? you weren't yourself for more than a few minutes, for longer than I want to remember, and the ectoplasm, disgusting, but what came after it, a manifestation of god knows what, a solid block of dark sugar with a head, arms and legs — I almost jumped out of my skin, Blanca, I could've had a heart attack! what were you thinking? were you trying to scare me, or just showing off? and Blanca, standing to her full height, which wasn't very tall right now, she'd climbed down to human proportions, no, *m'hija,* it was simply to show you what I'm capable of, so you'll show me some respect, and she turned her back on me.

At the edge of furious fury, wanting to put on a crazy act, I still couldn't get up off the chair but leaned forward as far as I could, saying, you mean to tell me, *mi querida amiga* — we were on intimate terms — you enjoyed scaring me, like there isn't a difference between witch or ghost in a state of enchantment and a majestic colonel or lowly soldier, Princes of Torture and Death, when it comes to recklessly frightening the life out of somebody — it could've been a real embarrassment, *mis amigos,* a sudden, involuntary contraction of the sphincter muscles, almost causing my bowels to release — no difference between the holy and spiritual world of the dead and the unavoidable, binding and suffocating power of the *Guardia Nacional,* the *Policía de Hacienda,* the *Policía Nacional?* a power they threw around, don't forget, with a vengeance, the crushing weight of fat bellies and bulging muscles landing on top of us with a shove here, a kick there, a torsional manipulation of arms and legs, a shattered skull if you weren't lucky, and Blanca, turning swiftly on her heels to reprimand me for crossing the line, an interruption that might've turned violent, who can say with these ghosts or witches, Blanca, shaking her head, her breath as hot as the fire in her eyes, don't exaggerate, just because I scared you, it doesn't mean you can say anything you want, you better watch what you're saying, *m'hija,* and your sweet Graciela Menéndez, a rung down on the ladder, I admit it was too much, comparing you to them, I'm sorry, *te debo una disculpa,* so I bowed my head, *mis amigos,* for having lost it, on account of being scared out of my wits by the *panela* with a head and arms and legs.

Antonio Aguilar, El Charro de México, singing another *ranchera,* "Antes que salga el lucero," the radio was laying it on thick for me, I was so happy to hear music that I forgot where I was for a minute, remembering my first love, taking shelter in his parents' shop on a rainy day, a radio playing a *ranchera,* a lot like but not "Antes que salga el lucero," my Flores brothers, with the same lighthearted horns, we were soaking wet from the rain, holding hands, and then we kissed, my first kiss, and José Matías and Wilber Eduardo, each lighting another cigarette, Wilber Eduardo, letting out a cough with a cloud of smoke, the Flores brothers, in one voice, you can tell us about it another time, it's not that we aren't interested, but you've got us wrapped up in one story and we don't have room for another, and Graciela Menéndez, offering another blinding smile, you're right, *mis amigos,* there's a time and place and this isn't it, so Blanca, she folded her hands, standing up straight, a little taller now, but nowhere near as tall as she'd been, saying, I forgive you, *m'hija,* look at this as an opportunity, there are people who don't concern themselves only with what transpires on the earth's surface, it's the inner reality that motivates, explains, and clarifies the irrational, hazardous events of our lives, there must be a reason for poverty, sickness, and death, for all the disagreeable things that bring sadness to our hearts, and you can't find the reasons on the earth's surface but in the soul — dreams are the means to see in one's soul or to see with one's soul.

Her words took me by surprise and sweetened the bitterness I'd tasted in my mouth on account of how much she'd scared me, and having gone so far as to say to her, a ghost, Blanca — because I was sure of it, no witch could become imperfectly transparent like she'd become after she spoke of dreams and the soul, but who knows! — that her behavior was looking a lot like the National Guard, Treasury Police, National Police, ORDEN, what a hot reception for my suspicions, what a talent for mistakes, what a change in exchange for a few kind words, I felt I was coming round to the opportunity standing in front of me, the opportunity was Blanca, and the *tihuilote* tree that would rise out of the floor — hysterical and historical thoughts were left behind and I really began to pay attention.

"Pobre corazón," written by Chucho Monge, played by Antonio Bribiesca, the radio was moving in a particular direction, tranquil — her tranquil gaze, the sea was tranquil — and his playing was pure genius, melancholy for a poor heart, but romantic, too, and a kind of concentration that went along with it, because I was ready to listen and to see, *mis amigos,* your Graciela Menéndez, Magic Menéndez was going to be my name, keep your eye on the rabbit, watch out for the hat, or the *tihuilote* tree, in this case, now that I was convinced she could do it, feeling the ecstasy of the moment that was about to begin, and full of desire, to see what Blanca was up to, lessons I couldn't learn at school, I count on my fingers and get there just as easily, and the unfeeling feeling of fear that assailed me not very long ago went up in smoke, the thunderstorm and rain blew it right out into the night, the quaking and shaking didn't stop but I got used to it, and Blanca, a messenger of sorts, a kind of pay-attention-to-me-and-you'll-learn-something, Blanca, a ghost of a different color, an unexpected truth.

José Matías and Wilber Eduardo, the Flores brothers, crushing out their cigarettes, leaning back against the thorny trunk of the tree, a silk-cotton tree, protecting them from the sun, leafy branches swaying in a light wind that caressed their faces, the Flores brothers, their eyes open wide on account of the story of the talisman, sitting a few yards away from the others, out of ear shot, and Concepción, Emiliano, Gustavo and Benavides, they didn't want to wait for them, impatience got the better of daylight, Concepción, Emiliano, Gustavo and Benavides waving, arms and hands, a kind of signal, we'll see you at home, we're on our way, *mis amigos,* and out of the corner of their eyes, a pair for each of them, Graciela Menéndez and the Flores brothers, José Matías and Wilber Eduardo, saw their friends leave with their arms full of leftovers, empty bottles of beer and soft drinks, greasy wrappers and paper bags, and Graciela

Menéndez, I see them but I won't look at them, playing with a strand of her hair, twirling it, not nervously, not distractedly, if I do I'll lose my concentration, the same concentration I was telling you about a minute ago — there are things that because they are such things are not to be done, like losing one's concentration, the single-minded pursuit of telling a story — so, just as I speak to you now with sought-after significance, I was staring then at Blanca with the eager eyes of one seeking an omen, an offering she'd make to my peaceful soul, a lead to follow, a lesson to learn, a woman, a ghost, who was going to conjure a *tihuilote* tree out of her very own floor.

Once upon a time there was a young woman named Graciela Menéndez, a young woman like almost any other young woman living in a small town with her mother and father and younger brother, Nelson, whom she called Segundo, for obvious reasons, and that was the sum of, the total of her family, united as they were in life, until the death of her younger brother many years later, which is a different story than the one I'm telling you now, my Flores brothers, just like other stories, *El Tabudo, El Cadejo,* the ghost, *Justo Juez,* mounted on his black horse, and *El Cipitío,* but this one, the one I'm telling you now, is my own story, and it's born out of the powers of Blanca, a ghost in a long line of conjure women, magic figures of the undead, maybe a witch at the same time as a ghost, why not, anything's possible in this world and the next, I won't make up my mind because, *mis amigos,* what's the point, better happy than right, and José Matías and Wilber Eduardo, relaxing against the trunk of the ceiba tree, a single voice, both of them saying at once, *¡A huevo!* and the light wind caressing them gave a gentle push against their faces, a sort of consensus of consensual friends, the three of them with three pairs of eyes, and the wind, too, waiting for the story of the talisman to go on, without a hitch, ending before sundown, at least, maybe with enough daylight left to find their way home, as if they needed the daylight to get there, which they didn't, it was their town, with the sun beating down, the flies pestering them, or the sun setting, it didn't matter, because they knew their way home with their eyes shut, the most natural thing in the world.

Blanca gathered together more than a handful of dried leaves, a few grains of corn, coffee beans, a glossy photograph of the Torogoz, a colorful, medium-sized bird of the motmot family, and a few sheets of coarse, colored paper out of her trunk, it was a bottomless trunk and must've held everything she'd taken with her to the next world, the place where she'd gone after death, and then she removed the thread from around her neck, with a small bird's skull and tiny beak, magic powers or good luck, it might've once been a hummingbird, I couldn't say, but definitely inhabited by a spirit, pointed and sharp, penetration and intimacy — vigor, energy, sexual potency — and she laid it on top of a particular sheet of colored paper, the kind children use to cut out shapes to make dolls or animals, construction or sugar paper, rough paper full of small particles of wood pulp you could see with the naked eye, but I couldn't see much in the flickering light from the kerosene lamp, so maybe this piece of sugar paper was a deep, soft violet color or purple, anyway it was a shade lighter and a color more vibrant than either gray or black. She didn't have her coins and magic powders, she didn't have her eyes shut, she didn't have a particular expression on her face, though it wasn't without expression, either, it was neutral but concentrating, and her lips were moving, pronouncing words that came to her from memory, and streaming out of her mouth at high speed without a sound, while the radio played softly in the background, "Celoso," sung by Los Panchos, and the lyrics were bittersweet, going along pleasantly with my mood, *mis amigos,* like the sound of rain falling from the sky, landing noisily on the roof of Blanca's shack.

> *Si no estás conmigo*
> *nada importa*
> *el vivir sin verte*
> *es morir.*
> *Si no estás conmigo*
> *hay tristeza*
> *y la luz del sol no brilla igual.*

> *Sin tu amor*
> *los celos me consumen*
> *y el temor no me deja dormir.*
> *Dime tú qué hago vida mía?*
> *Sin tu amor*
> *yo voy a enloquecer.*

Blanca, concentrating on what she was doing, laying out the sheets of rough, colored paper, arranging them according to a specific design in definite places on the floor required by her magic spell, based on precise colors, it seemed, as there was no single piece of paper that resembled any another, using her fingers to pinch and place dried leaves, a few grains of corn and coffee beans, three here, four or five there, each grain and bean, a different combination, an exact location on a sheet of colored paper, the dried leaves, grains of corn, coffee beans like points on a map, indicating a particular direction of the compass — if I'd had a compass to check it — and at last the photograph of the Torogoz, propped up in front of her, leaning against a small block of wood, maybe Cachimbo, sweet smelling, with combustible resin in its heart, like all of us in Our Republic of the Savior, combustible resin in our hearts, and finally the hummingbird skull, its pointed beak, a sort of pendulum, weight hanging from a fixed point so that it could swing freely backward and forward, she relaxed her wrist, wiggled her fingers, gave her wrist a brief, gentle massage with her left hand, then she picked up the thread with the skull and its sharp beak hanging from it, swinging it slowly steadily, her lips still moving, slowly steadily over the things she'd set out on the sheets of sugar paper, her eyes fixed on the photograph of the Torogoz, a medium-sized bird, knowing that what she'd removed from her trunk, in conjunction with the words she spoke silently to herself, would work to make a *tihuilote* tree rise out of the floor, and Blanca, repeating out loud, for my benefit, you'll love it, really, and it'll make your eyes water real tears of joy.

Rising up through the floor, not breaking the surface, but climbing up out of nowhere with Blanca's encouragement — she was gifted with a real brilliance, *un auténtico brillo* — pulling itself up, a sort of magic, enchantment not illusion, the tree reached upwards like a child that was green and brown, at first, and then its fingers were leaves, stretching its tiny arms that quickly became branches, inhaling the breath of life Blanca gave it, exhaling into the two-room shack, a *jacal,* if you want to call it that, but let's speak with respect, *mis amigos,* a living breathing *tihuilote* tree coming straight up out of something like a sheet of linoleum that had been placed on the trampled-down dirt, serving as a floor covering in Blanca's home.

José Matías and Wilber Eduardo, not exactly relaxed but leaning against the thorny trunk of the tree, Wilber Eduardo almost burning his fingers on the smoldering butt of a cigarette, not used to smoking, while José Matías, he wasn't thinking of lighting another Delta Red, sucked in by the story of the talisman, a silent crescendo of yelling and whistling paying tribute to the talisman, a waving of handkerchiefs before their eyes, the Flores brothers, astonished by what Graciela Menéndez was telling them, satisfied that she'd be able to help them, her experience with the unearthly, dreamy, spirit world, a unique adventure, the first but maybe not the last, Graciela Menéndez, the next step, a guide to what went on beneath the ceiba tree, the *Yaxché,* a refreshing and shady tree, connecting the planes of the underworld, *Xibalbá,* and the terrestrial realm and the skies, *Xibalbá,* where souls of the dead might rest and be in peace forever, there was information in experience you couldn't find in text books, not in church, either, a special sort of enlightenment, not found in *Diario Co Latino, El Diario El Mundo,* or *La Página,* and the window opening on the Flores brothers' soul, a shared soul of suffering, they weren't poker-faced but showed thoughtful expressions, remembering their own words, we felt the danger like a slicing wind, it's around the corner, or straight ahead, we don't know when or where it'll strike, like lightning, and in your story, they went on, together, speaking out loud, in your story, Graciela, there's lightning and thunder, so it's a sign, you're here to guide us, and Graciela Menéndez, pointing her finger at a silhouette in the near distance, a *urraca,* a kind of magpie with a blue breast and gray head, hopping across the rise of a hill, a rare bird, another sign for José Matías and Wilber Eduardo, a sign they would've missed if it weren't for Graciela Menéndez, Magic Menéndez, Our Savior of the Flores Brothers, storyteller and observer, who always pays attention to her surroundings, and no sooner had they seen it, the Flores brothers and Graciela Menéndez, the three of them — they could've clapped their hands but didn't want to frighten the bird — than the *urraca,* elegant, an expression of gracious living, took a hop, a leap that sent it at least six inches above the ground, and the magpie, landing softly, sank into the earth, volcanic soil, and disappeared like the sun sinking into the sea.

It was then I realized that the doubt I had thought eternal only a little while before was already gone, replaced by a profound faith, at least for the moment, in Blanca and her powers as a sorceress, a ghost, too, but a kind of miracle-worker — a living breathing *tihuilote* tree didn't define her limits but swung the door wide open on her other skills and likely countless accomplishments, *mis amigos,* and it was the thrill of my time on earth, up until that night, a night of lightning, thunder and rain, the final hours of the night and the early hours of the morning spent with my eyes wide open, like yours, right now, my Flores brothers, and getting a solid education, too, we all know how to make such good friends, don't we, and good things multiply, so Blanca was standing in a corner of the room, as far away from the window and the kerosene lamp as she could stand, a better view from there, the *tihuilote* tree, almost full grown, a young adult after a brief childhood — such is the way of all living things — Blanca grinning from ear to ear, her pride and joy, no cliché was too big, too well-fed for anyone at that very moment, and Blanca, a ghost or a witch with powers to conjure a living tree, out of a sheet of linoleum that was a floor covering in her home, I'd seen it with my own eyes, and I only had to wait in order to learn more from her, but that's another story, too, my Flores brothers, because we met half a dozen times in the years that followed, and I didn't tell anyone, not even you, if you'll forgive me — an intimate experience only stays that way if you don't speak about it, otherwise it'll go up in smoke — maybe I'm superstitious, call it whatever you want to call it, but that's the way it is, so now's the time to reveal the wonders of the world.

José Matías and Wilber Eduardo, not asking for more than what they were getting from her, the story of the *tihuilote* tree, clinging to the unknown with an eye on the future, we'll be as good as new with an experience like that in our lives! patience wasn't easy for the two brothers, their thoughts lying uneasily on the cold ground, living with a sense of dread, and a heavy cloud of stones hovering over their heads, the we-don't-know-when-or-where-it'll-strike following them like a whipped dog, and the cloud, threatening to throw a rain of stones down to crush them under its weight, the Flores brothers, you don't have to excuse yourself, *nuestro rey del dulce,* but please, you've got to continue, we know there's a message here in your words that'll guide us, and Graciela Menéndez, as beautiful as she was on the day they met her maybe forty years ago, Graciela Menéndez, serving up another smile, her perfect teeth, not like Nelson's, the brother she called Segundo, Graciela Menéndez, what was I saying, *mis amigos?* and looking up at the sky, José Matías offering his brother another cigarette, Wilber Eduardo refusing it, his throat was raw, they followed her gaze, the sun edged its way a little further down in the sky, definitely heading for the horizon, but you really had to pay attention, because it was a slow descent, gradual, nothing sudden, a relaxation of the background so fabricated they all thought someone must've been lowering the sun by using a pulley and a cord, the Flores brothers and Graciela Menéndez, together, eyes on the two-o'clock sun, and Graciela Menéndez, I'm laughing with you, my guiding lights, words that came out of her mouth, flying at the orbit of planets and the brilliant brilliance of stars, turning her head to look at the Flores brothers, now I know, *mis amigos,* that I'm looking at the *tihuilote* tree, almost full grown, and at Blanca, revealing a self-confidence bordering on a there-is-no-question, and a not-a-shadow-of-a-doubt, as she opened her mouth, almost transparent lips, I'm in charge of every one of my acts, acts over which I exercise enviable control and manipulation — we look for everything and its name — invigorated by my loss of breath, after an extended chill, at one time my death, *m'hija,* and I'm neither weak nor strong, it's a peculiar way of dealing with my condition, a ghost, a miracle for my neighbors and friends, tasting like funeral flowers, but a spark of life after death that's lighted in cases like mine, permitting the sort of magic you see before you now.

Blanca's generosity was beyond that of any living human being I'd met up to that night, a night in the blustering thunderstorm, of course I can't say my parents weren't generous, they gave us everything they could, but it was their loving duty toward Segundo and myself, so it didn't stand out the way Blanca's gift stood out to me, a generosity without rhyme or reason, at least I didn't understand it at first, but it was clear later on, and against a backdrop of overall selfishness, the world as it is, knowing her as I did for not more than an hour, it was a remarkable example of unselfishness — you remember, my Flores brothers, it was the first time I'd met her, and our following visits were in the years to come — so when I say she was generous to me it was a fact, she gave me a branch of the *tihuilote* tree, its flowers and fruit, food for various birds and bats, and Blanca, here, *m'hija*, take it, it's your souvenir, the leaves will stay green and live forever, like its flowers and fruit, and when I looked closely at it in the subdued light of the kerosene lamp, there wasn't a drop of sap, the tree's blood, where she'd separated it from the trunk, nothing to show for the operation, it wasn't a large branch, but a substantial remembrance which she reassured me would serve one day as a talisman, should I need it, while my fingers, touching the branch and trembling, caressing the living wood, felt my own life coursing through it.

I was still sitting in the chair she'd pointed at with her finger, a chair I hadn't seen but found by feeling my way in the room without banging into anything, *mis amigos,* scraping the soles of my shoes on something like a sheet of linoleum, serving as a floor covering, now broken open by the thunder-lightning-sparks-eurekas presence of a full-grown, living and breathing *tihuilote* tree, and Blanca, leaving me with my souvenir, an evolving, dawning talisman, a talisman budding like the compact, knoblike growths on the *tihuilote* tree that had already developed into flowers, blossoming right in front of my eyes, Blanca, walking to the kerosene lamp in the window whose flame was blocked out by a photograph, lifting the photograph in its frame — it'd been leaning there all this time, and I'd forgotten about it — she held the photograph above her head, her eyes shut, her lips moving, as before, but now I understood her words, and Blanca, as I lived when I was a little girl, and as a young woman, so I live today, but in a body that's no longer my own, yet resembles me — we don't change that much after death if we go on living — and you can see, *m'hija,* I have the same form, more transparent, of course, let's say I have the same shape, and definitely the same soul I always had in the years I was living, and your Graciela Menéndez, holding the branch in both hands, a talisman, looking up at Blanca, quoting a few words, "hardening without losing your tenderness," without boasting that I knew them, and Blanca, nodding, you're right, *m'hija,* they're good words and true, and the branch of this *tihuilote* tree, with its flowers and fruit will keep you from harm, you won't lose your tenderness, it's your talisman — don't be surprised, I know what you're thinking — it will love you and defend you to the death, like a sister, and Blanca, reaching into her heavy-looking trunk, digging around in it, a bottomless trunk, returning to me with something in her hand, always keep it wrapped in this, Blanca giving me a cloth made of a very soft material, it'll protect the talisman from all kinds of weather and temperatures, water, dirt and dust, and thieves will never hold it in their hands, the talisman will disappear right before their eyes, because only authorized hands, with your benediction and your permission, can touch it, now and forever, and like I said, its forceful first-rate flowers, fruits and green leaves will live for eternity.

Graciela Menéndez, Our Savior of the Flores Brothers, tied her story up with divine knots of sacred delight, a friend for life, Magic Menéndez offering the whereabouts of her talisman, buried long ago, to José Matías and Wilber Eduardo, who weren't asking anything of her, just the story, but Graciela Menéndez, you can have it, if you think it'll help you, *mis amigos,* I'll give you permission, beyond all scientific explanation, in the form I was taught by Blanca, the formulaic form of a formula, a recipe, a piping hot dish served to anyone wishing to use my talisman, and your burden shall be mine, your creeping suspicion, something hanging over your heads, that you can't describe but feel just the same, like a premonition, and Graciela Menéndez, clasping Wilber Eduardo's hand in hers, clasping José Matías' hand in hers, together, a hearty warmth passing through the skin of intimate friends, between Our Savior of the Flores Brothers and the Flores brothers themselves, wrists and palms and fingertips, contact points heating up that instantly warmed their hearts.

José Matías and Wilber Eduardo, riding in the pickup, heading toward San Ildefonso, thirteen kilometers north of *la Carretera Panamericana,* in the eastern sector of the Department of San Vicente, leaving behind Graciela Menéndez's story of the talisman, noted down forever in their brains, and the town of Lajas y Canoas, the shimmering mirage of Lajas y Canoas disappearing behind them now in the rearview mirror, and leaving behind their immeasurably popular Anastasio Aquino, but no, not yet, maybe a last glass of *aguardiente,* a *guaro* in the company of a king, one for the road, so to speak, and the two of them back at a table drinking *Tic tac* with the King of the Nonualcos, the Flores brothers, in a parallel world for another couple of minutes, just for a quick drink in the burning sunlight, what joy and relaxation! at a table with Anastasio Mártir Aquino, *Rey de los Nonualcos,* José Matías and Wilber Eduardo, together, on the train that wasn't a train with a locomotive but a train of thought, a train also carrying Anastasio Mártir Aquino, a distraction for the Flores brothers, and José Matías, a definitive gesture, raising his glass, saying, and this, our King, is a toast in your honor before we head back to our journey for the talisman — a long story we won't bore you with — a tribute to you, a thank-you-very-much for keeping us company, more than a distraction, an honor, and a real history lesson for us, while riding in the cab of our pickup truck, a lot of worrying on the road, you know how we are, my King, and Wilber Eduardo, raising his glass, saying to himself, I can handle one more, but no more than that or I'll pass out where I'm sitting and get a third-degree burn from this brutal sun, he was practically out of sorts, it must've been the heat, and in the other world, the riding-in-the-truck world, he wanted to get the talisman and finish the business they had with what they'd seen that scared the living daylights out of them, whereas his brother, José Matías, standing with a glass in his hand, loosening up with each *guaro,* a *Tic tac,* enjoying the heat of the sun and the company of a king, José Matías didn't seem to care how they passed the time while riding in the pickup, it was either remembering Graciela Menéndez's story or a visit with the King, so time passed quickly, but Wilber Eduardo the impatient one, and tired, too, enough of this daydreaming, I just want to get to San Ildefonso, find Graciela Menéndez's talisman, dig it up, and bury the past.

Anastasio Aquino, *Rey de los Nonualcos,* proud as a king, without showing it, but a friendly smile, a fitting salutation satisfied the leader in him, and a cool, refreshing glass of *aguardiente,* a *Tic tac* fortifying him against the unmerciful sun beating down from a pitiless white sky, a sort of dream to all who were present, Wilber Eduardo joining his brother, standing beside him, a toast, they raised their glasses, a *guaro* each, the Flores brothers and the King of the Nonualcos, the King remained seated, and together they downed their drinks.

Wilber Eduardo, it's nice and neat, the circle's complete, at least as far as the King of the Nonualcos is concerned, our *Rey de los Nonualcos,* reaching across the seat in the pickup to give his brother's shoulder a vigorous squeeze, José Matías lighting another cigarette, yes, it got us this far, and we're almost there, *mi hermano,* between Anastasio Aquino and the story of the talisman, a history lesson and a tale told by Graciela Menéndez, between these two things we aren't afraid of what we'd seen before we saw the horse, a neighing horse — I believe in the foolish primitivism of people who oppose reason with superstition — raising its head, lowering it, nodding like it was agreeing to something we were asking it with our eyes, maybe asking what was happening to us, the horse returning our looks without saying a thing, just nodding, and maybe, after all, it wasn't agreeing to anything, and Wilber Eduardo, you're right, *mi hermano,* it was nodding its head like any other horse, no secret messenger, no observer of the moon, now I can say it, words aren't illegal, and José Matías, inhaling and exhaling smoke, a bluish-gray cloud spinning as it went out the pickup's window.

The Flores brothers hadn't known then that the magic dogs, resting nearby in the shade of an evergreen shrub, the Mexican yew, weren't worrying or concerned at all that the Flores brothers were in trouble, a consensus, at least nothing urgent for José Matías and Wilber Eduardo, just a natural panic, something happening on the inside, while the hot sun and dry wind on the outside was pushing for a little sleep, a siesta was the right thing, so the *cadejos,* for a few minutes, closing their eyes, but right now, the magic dogs, wide awake and stretched out under a tarp in the back of the pickup, with a case of twelve-ounce cans of Kolashampan Bravo at hand, *siempre contigo,* the *cadejos,* always watching over the Flores brothers, always there under the circumstances, if there was a potential threat, where the sky and land met, and they were dedicated to protecting José Matías and Wilber Eduardo.

Half a day had slipped away, the Flores brothers, on the road, a slice of time gone by since José Matías and Wilber Eduardo were hiding behind a few boulders, crossing themselves, bowing their heads in a secret ancestral spell — an observer would've said they were shaking in their boots — peeking around the boulder, then mustering the courage, or it might've been impatience for a cigarette, José Matías and a Delta Red, they exposed themselves, fanning away the sweat that poured from their pores, José Matías leading the way, following in the hoof steps of a horse, climbing into the cab of their truck, and Wilber Eduardo's watch, a reliable present from Gustavo, an imitation because the original costs a fortune, ticking away the seconds, minutes and what seemed like hours they'd been on the road, passing Lajas y Canoas, a simple town on an average map, a savory spot of life that went by outside the pickup's window, not more or less important than any spot on a map, a wave and it was gone, they were moving on, San Ildefonso and the talisman in Graciela Menéndez's parents' backyard waiting for them, José Matías and Wilber Eduardo, in the sunny combustion of the same unnerving day, long released from the Pan-American Highway — more than 29,000 miles long — and heading north, don't look at your watch, *mi hermano,* we're almost there, and in a couple of minutes, a wild conception of reality, maybe a few seconds but don't count them, and the Flores brothers, arriving at last where they were headed, the pickup truck cruising into the heart of San Ildefonso, the sun still high in the sky, spilling its own candescence, pouring its hope on top of them, slumped ever so slightly toward the horizon, not much, measuring the distance it had slumped in its sky-blue chair, the width of an index finger if you held it up to the heavens, it wasn't nearly enough to bring the slightest cool breeze of the evening out of hiding, it was far too early, and not nearly enough to allow the Flores brothers to lift their sunglasses, large metal Ray-Ban Aviators, from their eyes; and at once, upon arrival, cruising into the heart of San Ildefonso, with a solution in sight, the talisman, they found their way to being what a man should be under the circumstances, and in a certain place: their own.

The town welcomed them, invisible open arms taking precious care of the truck and the Flores brothers riding in the cab, almost carrying them, and not a sound out of the two brothers, not a word, a breath definitely, they were breathing easily after such a brief long journey with something like a ghost or monster right out of a Mexican horror movie trailing right behind them, and the *cadejos,* too, they didn't look up at more than what they could see from the edge of the tarpaulin, they knew San Ildefonso like they knew every inch of their country whether they'd been there or not, intimate knowledge with all that lived, breathed and grew on the land, the magic dogs, stretching their legs — instead of paws, they had hooves like a deer — staring at a slightly slumping sun in a white sky pouring hot sunlight on a couple of what looked like dogs' noses sticking out from under the edge of the tarp where it was tied down against the wind.

José Matías, his peripheral vision working on the left side of the road, trying to find the turn that would take them to

Graciela Menéndez's parents' house, it was definitely a left he'd have to take, following directions he'd been given that were printed on paper in his memory, sign on the dotted line, and it's all yours, the directions were in his memory exactly as Graciela Menéndez had given them to him, like a signature scrawled on a legal document, written in memory's ink on memory's paper from a day not so long ago when Graciela Menéndez had told them the story of the talisman and where to find it, buried in the yard behind her parents' house.

Wilber Eduardo was craving a pure and cold drink, he'd finished the syrup from a jar of Miguel's Changungas, after he'd eaten the nance fruit, and there were half a dozen vacuum-sealed plastic bags of one hundred percent natural San Andrés brand *Jocote rojo* and a couple of leftover jars of Miguel's Changungas on the floor beneath the dash, but the syrup with nance fruit wasn't cold, and the *xocotl,* the fruit, bittersweet, was the same temperature as the air around them; he really wanted a tall glass of beer or at least a horchata flavored with black morro seeds, nutmeg and cinnamon — Wilber Eduardo, rubbing his hands together, now that we're here I could really use a Pilsener, what do you say, *mi hermano,* do we stop for a beer? and José Matías, straightening the wheel, it wasn't a bumpy road, reaching with his right hand for a half-empty pack of Delta Reds, when we get our hands on the branch of that *tihuilote* tree, with its flowers and fruit, our talisman and a gift from Graciela Menéndez, then we can talk about a drink, until then, keep your eyes on the road, a navigator is what we need right now, or it'll be an ambulance if I drive off the road because

I'm looking for the right turn, a left, and the right house, and José Matías, a cigarette between his lips, shooting a glance at his brother, with a smile on his face, the pickup went past a school painted deep-ocean blue, and Wilber Eduardo, I can wait, I agree, it's a relief we've arrived in one piece, or two, I guess, *mi hermano,* all joking aside, it's been a long day that isn't over and a long journey to go with it.

Graciela Menéndez, Our Savior of the Flores Brothers, describing the house with great care for details to help them find it and the talisman, with her permission, if they ever needed it, hadn't counted on weather and time and the changes they put on the appearance of things after a few years, wind and rain, neglect, and the sweltering heat of the sun, and her parents didn't live in San Ildefonso anymore to take care of the backyard and whatever grew in it or was buried there.

Despite the changes brought on by weather and time, with Wilber Eduardo serving as navigator, José Matías, after spelling out in detail the directions Graciela Menéndez had given him, he was the pilot, pulled the truck off the road a few yards away from what had to be the house that belonged to Graciela Menéndez's parents, deserted, almost forbidding, not very large, like the other houses they'd passed on the way, but a real house, not a shack, small as it was, with holes in the roof that must've let in plenty of rain during the season of rain, and a lot of ants, more than a few rats, maybe an entire colony of Alfaro's rice rats, and other medium-sized creatures, an iguana, but a tapir couldn't get in through the front door, each creature looking out for a safe place to eat and sleep without being bothered by a living soul, a mortal, walking on two legs, a resident of San Ildefonso.

Wilber Eduardo, giving the house the once-over, reciting to himself, *Entonces ves este país, / que puede ser del tamaño de un raspón,* a line from Alfonso Quijada Urías, then to his brother, you're sure this is it, it's a run-down place with nothing to hide from anybody climbing in through an un-locked window, and José Matías, throw me a pack of ciga-rettes, a full one, from the glove compartment, we'll see if there is an unlocked window or not, and we don't need a flashlight, the sunlight's pouring through holes in the roof, the Flores brothers walking right up to the front door, but Wilber Eduardo, there's no way to get in, walking away from his brother to peer in a window bolted shut without shutters against the sun, and from here I can't see very much, just that it's a mess in there, and José Matías, standing beside him, you can say that again, I wonder why they left it like it is without coming to check on it, at least now and then, it isn't like it's far away, but Graciela must've — and inter-rupting his brother, Wilber Eduardo, let's go around the back, it's the backyard we're looking for, isn't it?

An untended backyard with low-lying, long dry and some-times green grass, hunched over and weakened, woven around fallen broken branches, a bird's nest rocked off the branch of a tree by high winds, a bicycle wheel and tire, the wheel rusted, the tire flat, drained of air, green grass under a Black Sapote, an evergreen tree, or a dangerous-looking Bullhorn Acacia, with its ants, trees hoarding groundwater, offering a little shade, or maybe a tall *maquilishuat,* an oak tree, wearing pink, a hummingbird, the sultry sun beating down, and San Ildefonso, a population living at more than 672 feet, the plants and trees, fed by the sometimes limpid, sometimes murky far-reaching Río Lempa and the waters of a reservoir, the Embalse 15 de Septiembre, watering what grew from the earth in the backyard of Graciela Menéndez's parents' house when there wasn't any rain.

José Matías and Wilber Eduardo, squinting in the sunlight, eyes fixed on a gently sloping hill and a small single-story building of simple and crude construction, maybe a shelter for animals, or a workshop, woodshed, tool shed, garden shed, a shed for storing grain, and the Flores brothers, standing without moving, frozen on the spot, looking at the dry and green grass and resolute trees that disguised the earth and a likely hiding place for the talisman the Flores brothers couldn't even begin to imagine finding without the help of magic or a dowsing rod, the blue sky and white-hot sunlight pressing down on them, and the talisman, wrapped in a cloth made of very soft material, a branch of the *tihuilote* tree, with its flowers and fruit, Wilber Eduardo, we'll never find it, I'm feeling sick, *mi hermano,* covering his face with his hands, ignoring the sweat running past his ears, and José Matías, handing him a handkerchief, take off your sunglasses and wipe your face, it looks worse than it is, looking away from his brother at the untended backyard, maybe we ought to pray or something, and Wilber Eduardo, or something like cry, *mi hermano,* and a dog started to bark in a neighbor's yard, a Black-collared Hawk flew above their heads, the Flores brothers, hearing screaming whistles, "hieeee," then nothing at all, José Matías and Wilber

Eduardo looking up, a piercing blue sky, the Black-collared Hawk, its warm color, chestnut-cinnamon plumage, black shaft streaks on the back, and a short, hoarse, raspy "eh-rrr" sounding in their ears, the hawk soaring off high above them in the roasting heat of the sun, heading in the direction of the languid Lempa.

The *cadejos,* white magic dogs wide awake and looking at the Flores brothers, at precisely the moment they were making up their minds, not about whether they should start looking but how to start looking, it wasn't going to be easy, more like impossible, and the word impossible didn't mean anything to the magic dogs, standing in the backyard, the Flores brothers couldn't see them, but they did see, with their eyes shut, printed on the lids, the never-ending rains being unleashed over the tranquility of graves, of friends and strangers who were just like friends, of all who'd died, all together we sing, thought Wilber Eduardo, but there really wasn't a place, no room for a micro-fissure of sarcasm, not a word or splinter of a word, so Wilber Eduardo, gathering his courage, reaching for his brother's arm, lacing his own through the space made friendly by the bent elbow of José Matías' arm, the Flores brothers, together, without knowing the magic dogs were already on the scent, José Matías and Wilber Eduardo headed toward the patch of green grass under a Black Sapote.

It wasn't the Black Sapote, but the savage-looking Bullhorn Acacia, with its ants, that drew the magic dogs, nimble on their hooves, sauntering right past the shuffling, inquisitive Flores brothers, José Matías and Wilber Eduardo, certain in their uncertainty, and persuaded by despair that there was nothing they could do to hasten the discovery of the talisman in such a hostile environment. The *cadejos,* sniffing around the Bullhorn Acacia, more than thirty feet tall, hollowed-out, swollen thorns in pairs at the base of its leaves, where colonies of stinging ants lived, ants fending off insects, curious mammals and epiphytic vines — no alkaloids for this tree — ants protecting the tree of its threatening trinity — in return, mutualism — and the magic dogs, if they could talk, the Flores brothers would've heard them say, here it is, we'll dig it up, but there was no need to speak, bark or howl, the magic dogs, with a skill reserved for the Blessed, digging with deerlike hooves, throwing clumps of earth and long blades of green grass behind them, a simple task, the talisman buried like a bone, and the Flores brothers, José Matías and Wilber Eduardo, hearing nothing but the return of the Black-collared Hawk, its screaming whistles, "hieeee," voices that couldn't guide them in their search, the Flores brothers on their hands and knees, without a magnifying glass, scrutinizing the earth with their eyes, holding their Ray-Bans in a free hand, off balance, nearly toppling over, while in the meantime, the *cadejos,* "we've got it," of course they didn't say a word, each taking one end of cloth with their teeth, muzzles buried in the earth, backward steps to extract themselves and the talisman, continuing to walk backward, dragging hope after them in their slow pace in the form of the talisman, hope for the Flores brothers, a talisman wrapped in cloth made of a very soft material to protect it from all kinds of weather and temperatures, water, dirt and dust.

The *cadejos* dropped the talisman in front of José Matías and Wilber Eduardo, within reach of their authorized hands, an object wrapped in soft cloth, the Flores brothers, eyes like saucers, eyes saying what the fuck! out of the blue! thinking of Graciela Menéndez and saying out loud, with your benediction and your permission, we can touch it, your talisman, made of these eternal, forceful first-rate flowers, fruits and green leaves, we've got a chance now, *mi hermano,* and Wilber Eduardo, looking up at the sky, a silent prayer of thanks crossing his lips, his brother, we should pick it up, but I'm afraid I'm dreaming, and Wilber Eduardo, all at once the stronger brother, we aren't dreaming, *mi hermano,* the world is like it is, but we've been offered a gift by Our Savior of the Flores Brothers, Wilber Eduardo reaching for the talisman wrapped in cloth, cradling it like a baby, and the magic dogs, climbing under the tarp in the bed of the truck, every day must come to an end, and we've earned our day, even though we're used to the night, no words between *cadejos,* but if the Flores brothers could've heard them, and José Matías and Wilber Eduardo, sweating bricks because now they had to follow through with it, their plan, and it gave them a shiver that ran the length of their spines, facing life isn't easy, *mi hermano,* Wilber Eduardo shaking his head, and José Matías, reclaiming his place in the hierarchy, don't tell me you're just seeing it now? after all we've been through, and maybe Reyes Vehemente, his polished boots, or José Enrique Embustera, and Wilber Eduardo, you know I wasn't like this before they arrested and beat us, dragged us off to jail, my brain is like a melon that's been too long in the sun, *mi hermano,* and José Matías, *perdóname,* putting his arm over his brother's shoulder, drawing him near, stroking the cloth covering the talisman with his calloused hands.

The pickup bounced along the uneven surface of the road, now heading southwest, the truck traveling with the wind chasing after it toward CA1, the Pan-American Highway, retracing the path the Flores brothers had taken to get the talisman from Graciela Menéndez's parents' backyard, the sun a little further down in the sky, the hood and roof of the cab roasted from the sun, a yellowish-haze of dust rising from the landscape around them, or it might've been their imagination, and the *cadejos* sleeping soundly side by side, the world seemed brighter to José Matías and Wilber Eduardo, with the talisman wrapped in cloth on the seat between them, paying little attention to the miles flying by without sensing the leaden weight of time, a drag on their souls, a kind of anticipation that'd made the journey to San Ildefonso take so long, like all traveling by car or truck on road journeys where the outcome is unknown, it was the going, not the returning that seemed to make time stand still, or at least left the Flores brothers with the feeling that the clock went on ticking, went on and on forever without time getting them anywhere, so Wilber Eduardo, thoughtful, remembering a line from a poem, reciting it to his brother with the accompaniment of rushing wind through the open windows, "We got off at the next-to-last station, your coat smelling of cold soup, / we spoke among other things of our country and the struggle for its liberation," and Wilber Eduardo, a memory like a trap when it came to poetry, it's Alfonso Quijada Urías, I was thinking of him, *mi hermano,* when we pulled up to the house, and José Matías, don't you think I know that? we went to the same school, not for very long, and today, every day and night, we read the same books — I always know what's on your mind, and Wilber Eduardo, slumping against the seat, half the country dying and the other half getting ready, lowering his head, a brick of depression smack in the face, now that they got what they were looking for, the Flores brothers, on their way with the talisman to the exact spot where they'd seen what frightened them, the winning ace in their hands, but Wilber Eduardo, not his brother, suffering from a debilitating condition, it was called accomplishment, a kind of defeat, you get what you're looking for, what you want, and then what? so he sat up straight, stuck his head out the window, turning his face to the wind, a refreshing freshness lifted his low spirits, returning his head and its tangled long hair into the cab, no longer slicked back with Vaseline and Brylcreem, the wind had tousled it, running fingers through his hair, a comb was an instrument for those who had one, and a pair of calloused hands that came to rest in his lap.

There wasn't any time on the return trip for a visit to the village where they'd had a meal with Rogelio and his mother, Mama Lola, they wanted to use the magic of the talisman right away on the ghost or monster they'd seen, something straight out of a Mexican horror movie, there wasn't enough time for a friendly visit to anyone, since time itself was in a hurry, running far ahead of the sun-burned roof and hood of the pickup, painted metallic-red but faded like it was sunburned, the bed of the truck covered by a tarp, and the *cadejos,* traveling under the tarp out of the sunlight but sweating, not really sweating, but their tongues were hanging out, their noses poking out for air from under an edge of the tarpaulin, and the Flores brothers, José Matías and Wilber Eduardo, no matter how fast time was racing, they kept up with it, the engine of the pickup tuned to perfection, retracing the path they'd set down on their way to San Ildefonso.

Their destination was roughly a quarter mile from where they'd been hiding behind some really big rocks, a quarter mile from the *tempisque,* and plenty of other trees, *tihuilote* trees, but not a big balsam with a wide smile, they were far away from the western Pacific coast, trees standing only two hundred yards away, which would've given plenty of shade to anyone who'd bothered to run an extra two hundred yards, but not the Flores brothers, they'd been out of breath, scared out of their wits, completely unnerved, with chests heaving, gulping for air, another breath and another inch of uneven land covered by unsteady legs and their lungs would've burst under thin, permanently bruised skin, and right now, a destination not far from San Esteban Catarina, the Flores brothers, on their way to a spot roughly a quarter mile away from where they'd seen a neighing horse, raising its head, lowering it, and the silence of the sky, it was early in the day but hot as hell, until at last they found the courage to get out from behind the boulders — not far away, barbed wire and a stone fence, they could've crouched on the other side of the stone fence, but they'd ducked behind some big rocks — the horse, turning its back on them, walking away, not in a hurry, no trot, gallop, pace or canter, and José Matías and Wilber Eduardo, hearing the clock ticking, the weight of time and a matter of life and death, getting up from behind the stones, walking to the pickup truck, following in the hoof steps of the horse, who kept on nodding its head as if to say you're heading in the right direction, don't turn back, my brothers; they got themselves out of there as fast as the engine and the wheels of the pickup truck would take them.

Give me a cigarette, José Matías prodding his brother, the pack's empty, check the glove compartment, and he crumpled the empty pack and threw it on the floor, the strong wind streaming through the open windows twirling the cellophane and paper, tossing it out the window on Wilber Eduardo's side, and Wilber Eduardo, opening the glove box, a single unopened pack of Deltas, no menthol for José Matías, every bump in the road a familiar bounce, José Matías, we've traveled this road before, and Wilber Eduardo, no fooling, *mi hermano,* it could've been minutes but it's been hours, tearing open the pack of Deltas, knocking a cigarette out of the top, putting the pack in front of his brother's face, and José Matías, taking one, thank you, I need a smoke, lighting up, smiling at Wilber Eduardo, watching the road, speaking softly, not hours, *mi hermano,* maybe a single hour, maybe less — and watch the talisman doesn't fly out of the truck, we're making time and the wind's trying to beat us there, and another strong gust of wind in the cab, maybe directly from heaven, reminding them who was in charge, giving them looks that could be translated as I'll be there before you can say Francisco

Valencia of *Diario Co Latino,* the Flores brothers and the truck retracing their drive and rolling straight for San Esteban Catarina, set on a lush hill, a *cerro,* the high land of San Esteban Catarina, a municipality in the department of San Vicente, Wilber Eduardo gently resting a calloused hand on the cloth covering the branch of the *tihuilote* tree, its flowers and fruit, food for various birds and bats, leaves that'll stay green and live forever, it'll keep them from harm and destroy the powers of what frightened them, a monster or ghost right out of a Mexican horror movie, the Flores brothers, no longer trembling with fear, a current of excitement coursing through them, and José Matías' pickup truck caught in the tailwind of a swift and saintly current of air carrying a flock of noisy parrots in the sky above them.

The Flores brothers, already traveling west on the Pan-American Highway, CA1W, the two-lane *Calle Panamericana,* José Matías and Wilber Eduardo passing the town of Chanmoco, a transmission tower reaching up at the blue sky, a blur as the burnt-red pickup went past it shoved onward by the high-speed warm wind and the weight of José Matías' foot on the accelerator, the journey going faster than the wind whistling in the trees, when you know what you've got to do and you're going to do it, Wilber Eduardo said out loud, and José Matías, nodding his head, an agreement without a handshake, a bond between them that was stronger than the bond of blood — no one can stare death in the face and then continue along the same path as if nothing had happened — brothers' blood tied together with their suffering, the Flores brothers savagely tortured during interrogations, maybe the National Guard, the Treasury Police, National Police, ORDEN, split skulls, broken ribs, popping eyes out with a spoon, generator-electricity, cigarette burns, a cigar now and then — the works — executions in prison, executions in the cemetery, massacres, and more death, how many? maybe seventy-five thousand killed, and six to eight thousand disappeared over a twelve-year period, fear tearing you apart, a real sin, not one of those things you say when you mean that it's a shame, but a sin that goes straight to heaven, written in a book up there for everyone to read, the Flores brothers, and a dead body, a man or a woman but not a child, they couldn't forget the horror they'd seen and smelled, the stinking body burnt to a crisp, maybe the body was alive when it was set on fire, the smell of that once-was-a-living-human-being that would stay with them for the rest of their lives, no fragrant *resedo* flowers falling like tears from the sky, real tears, and plenty of them, but today, right now, a talisman as a tool of justice in their hands, a righteous pair of brothers, José Matías and Wilber Eduardo, on their way to put right an act of evil reborn for them in the form of a threatening ghost or monster, something straight out of a Mexican horror movie, but it wasn't a movie at all, they'd seen what had frightened them with their own eyes, José Matías and Wilber Eduardo, the noble Flores brothers, law-abiding and principled, on their way to protect themselves and purify a soul tainted with evil, a magic talisman in their hands, a gift from Graciela Menéndez, the Flores brothers carrying deep within their hearts no shadow of a doubt that this path was their destiny.

Graciela Menéndez, with honey-sweet and tender words, and vision like a soothsayer, a sage or clairvoyant, without examining the entrails of animals, confiding in Emiliano, not everything, but more or less the whole story with the exception of the talisman, Concepción turning the pages of a magazine, listening not reading, ears like a jaguar, smoking a cigarillo, Concepción, Concha, pretending to ignore them while looking at the pictures, and Lucía sitting next to Emiliano, taking his hand in hers, Gustavo standing at the window, drinking a Fanta Orange, Graciela saying, they're angels, our Flores brothers, you know it and I know it, and they never collapsed under the weight of what they went through, not on the outside, but the damage inside, *mis amigos,* like all of us, who can see the damage inside us from the outside? and Emiliano, frowning, except for scars and missing fingers or a single eye, interrupting her with a compassionate voice, and Concepción, wait a second, El Puño, she always called Emiliano the Fist, but Lucía, whispering his name, Leo, squeezing his hand, and Concha, I'm thinking of Benavides, fucked up by the National Guard, the murder of three hundred farmers on the banks of Río Sumpul in Chalatenango, scars you can't see, maybe on his scalp, but his brain, knocked loose, it's always the birds and the bees for Benavides, her sweet joke, but everyone wanting to cry, a pain they shared, and Lucía, the earth stained with blood leaked out of skin suffering and dying, what can we do about it? those who did it, who tortured and killed us, aren't likely to show up here to face trial, and Graciela reaching for a sugary coffee in a mug, a sigh that had some hope in it, maybe faith in the ruling of a North American judge, she'd read the decision too, Graciela's belief in justice, in this life or the next, and a lot of prayers, a Catholic speaking to God, Graciela, putting down her mug, sitting back against the cushions, with our worries and unconsumed but consuming fears we'll only find solace in praying for our Flores brothers, that their task will be fulfilled — with heroism, balls, guts and spunk — maybe even freeing each of us into the bargain, our prayers will be answered through them, José Matías and Wilber Eduardo, and Emiliano, nodding his head, a sigh like a hiss that slipped out from between his pursed lips, and then a question, did they tell you what they'd seen, what it's all about? Graciela shaking her head no, it was something they couldn't put in words, a horror they couldn't name, a presentiment, so to calm my spirit — I could only imagine the worst, a return of something or someone so threatening as to endanger us all — I put myself in their place, mentally projecting myself into them and trying to understand their sensitivity, and when I found that place and settled in there, I understood they had to do what they were going to do, whatever it was — one of the problems that really is a problem — and they were doing it for us, too, it is our only hope, and Lucía, they're no more sensitive to the past and present than we are, but how can we help them now when we couldn't help ourselves then? how can we help ourselves now when we couldn't help them then? because it's the same thing, then and now, now and then, when it comes to fright, when it comes to being afraid, we're locked in a closet of fear, and Concepción, Concha, closing the magazine, her silence louder than words, but at last, looking straight at her friends, with a commanding voice, that's exactly the point, it's the same thing, whether it's José Matías and Wilber Eduardo, or you Graciela, Emiliano and Lucía, and Concepción, turning her head toward the window, looking at Gustavo, a can of Fanta in his hand, and convincing Concepción's persuading voice, her words flying out of her mouth, and you Gustavo, and our mothers and fathers, sisters and brothers, our neighbors, strangers, we're all the same, it's up to us to do what we can, and the Flores brothers are doing it for us, an effort to retroactively rectify the situation, today, and maybe for the rest of our lives, and Concepción, taking in a lungful of smoke, exhaling in Gustavo's direction, Gustavo ducking and weaving, grinning, you're a dynamic and determined stick of dynamite, conjuring a line almost straight out of *Casablanca*, Concha, getting back at her on account of the smoke, and Concepción, blowing him a warmhearted kiss, a maternal smile, remembering how Gustavo had given Wilber Eduardo a watch as a birthday present, an imitation, the original costs a fortune, Gustavo couldn't afford a real one, but it's the best imitation you can buy, Graciela, Emiliano and Lucía, Concepción, Gustavo, Benavides, and the Flores brothers, a big family, branches springing from a single root, with heights to scale, shedding fears of the past, purging themselves of anxiety and foreboding, you can go on living but life is never the same, we're carrying our past like a burro carries the burden of its master, and now that Concepcíon was finished speaking, she lowered her eyes, drew on the cigarillo hanging from between her lips, filled her lungs, let out a bluish-gray cloud of smoke, and Emiliano, I just hope it works, whatever you've told them, Graciela, and Lucía and Gustavo and Concepción nodding their heads in agreement, and Graciela, who kept the story of the talisman to herself, she gave them everything but that part of the Flores brothers' story, something she didn't tell anyone else about, only letting José Matías and Wilber Eduardo in on it, another bond between them, like two brothers and a sister, at least not telling anyone else that she'd given the Flores brothers an object thought to have magic powers, a real belief on her part, until she had the result of their mission and the talisman back in her hands.

Gustavo going to the kitchen to throw away the empty can of Fanta, Emiliano following him there, leaving the three women on their own, Lucía joining Graciela on the sofa, Concepción staying where she was, smoking her cigarillo, but leaning forward, getting as close as she could to the other two, whispering, I've got a variation on a tale, involving a strangler fig, a wild fig tree known as *higuera* and *higuerón,* as well as *matapalo,* tree-killer, maybe you know it, *mis amigas,* because we know it as *amate,* Aztecs and Maya used its bark, the bark of native strangler figs, to make a kind of paper for the original Mexican codices, the paper's called *amatl* in Náhuatl, *copo* in Mayan — the outer bark makes darker paper, the inner bark usually makes lighter paper — and it's best cut, my sisters, in the spring, when it's new and causes less damage, and *amate* is also cut into human or animal forms for witchcraft rituals, then buried in front of the person's house or an animal enclosure, and Concepción, Concha with a hot whisper, inviting curiosity, Graciela and Lucía all ears, Concha saying softly, and each species of fig depends on its own species of pollinating fig wasp, so when the tree is covered with tiny green figs, thousands of these wasps appear, attracted, I guess, by a scent released by the tree or the figs, and female wasps, pollen pockets already filled to capacity — the place is jam-packed with pollen — proportions we can only imagine, female wasps enter the young fig by wiggling through a tiny hole in its apex, and as they do so, they lose their antennae and wings, now I've seen everything! and once inside, the female wasps pollinate the stigmata in each fig, generous trees and charitable wasps — but what am I saying? *mis amigas,* my story has nothing to do with bark or paper or wasps, even though our fig trees are mentioned in poetry and romance, and they're part of daily life, thought of with affection, to say the least, and to put it mildly, our *amate,* without a voice of give-me-what's-mine, never selfish, they go fifty-fifty on joining their lives with ours, in the hearts of women and men and children, but my story isn't a long story, the variation I'm going to tell you takes a little longer than it'd take to read, and Graciela, comfortable on the sofa, folded her hands in her lap, while Lucía, tilting her head to rest it on the cushion, shut her eyes, both women listening to Concha, and Concepción, content with a small audience, lit another cigarillo.

Gustavo, the empty can of Fanta crushed and lying in a recycling bin, Graciela Menéndez, thinking of everything, doing her best for the environment, and Emiliano, Leo, sitting on a kitchen chair, he'd turned it around and was leaning forward with his arms hanging over the backrest, daydreaming, they'd left the three women on their own in the other room, Graciela, Lucía and Concepción, and Emiliano looking up, snapping out of it, what do you think, Gustavo, of what the Flores brothers are up to? and Gustavo, rinsing a glass in the sink, opening the refrigerator looking for something to drink, I'm dying of thirst, Leo, it must've been the *shuco* I drank, and the rice tortillas with avocado and cheese I couldn't stop eating, I can't think when I'm thirsty, and Gustavo, filling a glass of water from a pitcher, swallowing the entire glass full of water, wiping his mouth with a dishcloth, putting the pitcher back in the refrigerator, what were you saying? yes, the Flores brothers, according to Graciela, and what she says is gospel to me, to all of us, José Matías and Wilber Eduardo will do what they can for us, but I'm not holding my breath, *mi querido amigo,* not after what we've been through, a repetition or a variation on a theme, ok, we've all said it, and I'll say it again, the fucking suffering, Leo — and Emiliano, interrupting him, what Concha said, the birds and the bees for Benavides, if we wanted an example, we've got one, a suffering that lasts, brain damage, but who wants an example? nobody wants a fucking example for fucking suffering, all you've got to do is look around at the ghosts walking the streets, working the land, you or me, and then there's the really dead ones, the ones that are buried with a headstone if they're lucky or washed down a river or burnt to a crisp or rotting somewhere under a pile of rocks, and nothing, that's what we've got, Emiliano waving his arms over the back of the chair, reaching at nothing with his outstretched hands, so I pray for the Flores brothers, ok? if I can pray at all, which, more than once since it happened — it being what we went through in the past, a thousand years ago, but really, it isn't that long ago or far away — I've asked myself plenty of times, God or no God at all, but I believe in Him, faith isn't in appearances, a phony or a fake which is a swindle on your soul, you can bet on it, my guts've been ripped out but I believe in God, and Gustavo looking at Emiliano, and Emiliano, red in the face, the color of a blood vessel about to burst, Gustavo putting his hands on Emiliano's shoulders, shaking him gently, squeezing the shoulders that were almost trembling, take it easy, brother, you'll give yourself a heart attack.

Concepción, a cigarillo between her fingers, head surrounded by a bluish-gray cloud of smoke, sitting with her captive audience, Lucía and Graciela Menéndez, Concepción, in a voice that was whispering, *Ma aca cacizquia noyol ac?* ayyo / *Zan yuh niyaz, / xochihuiconticac ye noyolio,* ayyo — Is anyone there who will become the owner of my heart? / Alone I must go, / my heart covered with flowers, and Lucía and Graciela, their eyes filled with tears at the poetry, understanding both the Náhuatl and the translation, but wondering where she was going with it, and Concepción, a quick bright look in her eyes, sharp witted and exhaling another cloud of smoke, I bet you're wondering why I'm reciting a bit of poetry, *mis amigas,* and Lucía and Graciela, you must've read our minds, Concha, the forest's getting pretty thick and we don't see where we're going, and it's a shame, Concha, the landscape is beautiful, the stage set by a few words of a poem by Tlaltecatzin, of Cuauhchinanco, a cultural and political tributary of Texcoco, near the end of the fourteenth century — you see, we've done our homework — a shame because you've got something to say so you should say it, and Lucía, picking up a glass, taking a sip, putting the glass down, and Graciela Menéndez, still comfortable on the sofa, but her hands were no longer folded in her lap, her fingers played with the fringe on a hand-woven blanket neatly folded beside her on the sofa.

The sunlight pouring down from the sky was beginning to fade into a yellowish-orange glow as the sun crept without being seen toward the horizon, and Concepción, now sitting straight in her chair, not whispering but pronouncing each word with the articulate articulation of a speech therapist, Graciela and Lucía listening with their eyes wide open, their ears were pricked, Concepción saying, our *amate* is a very popular tree in El Salvador, its trunk is very thick, its branches look like claws, it doesn't have flowers and it doesn't bear fruit, and amongst its misshapen branches lies a secret — do you know what that secret is, *mis amigas?* and Concepción, taking a lungful of smoke and exhaling it into the air above her, a cloud drifting upward, hovering beneath the ceiling, I'll tell you where it begins, where we can begin to uncover the secret, it's in a legend about the wicked appearance of our *amate,* a folk tale, mythology, a fable that says, at midnight, a beautiful white flower blooms at the top of the *amate* tree — the branch with a white flower, the branch with a single flower — and falls, maybe it falls slowly like a leaf tossing and turning in the waves of a windless night, falling from the magic *amate* tree, a wild fig tree known as *higuera* and *higuerón,* as well as *matapalo,* tree-killer, and if you catch the flower, you'll have everything you want, love, money and health, but it isn't so easy, there's always an obstacle, and Graciela sighing, nervously fingering the fringe on a hand-woven blanket, and Lucía, holding out a hand worth holding out in front of her, looking at her fingernails, asking a simple question, shaping the words with a provocative pair of lips — the advantage is the attraction, the disadvantage is the attraction — a pair of lips exotic and traditional, eternal and folkloric lips like the rhythm of a dance known as *Xuc,* a dance to the song "Adentro Cojutepeque," ask any man who'd seen her before Emiliano, and Emiliano marrying her straight away, nobody's fool, and Lucía's enchanting mouth asking, why isn't it simple, Concha, to catch the flower if it's tumbling down weightless from the top of an *amate* tree on its way to the ground? and Concepción, clearing her throat even though there was nothing in it to clear away, Graciela lifting her hand from the blanket and wiggling her fingers, what is it, Concha? and Concepción, zeroed in on her thoughts, concentrating on her words, according to the legend, in order to catch the flower, and that's the point, I've made it clear, you must first have a deadly fight with the Devil, who's the owner of the flower — to butter you up, tell me now don't tell me later — and if the Devil wins he steals your soul, but if you win and catch the flower, solitary and white, hips swaying as it floats down, down, down, then fame, fortune, love and health will be yours for eternity, and according to some villagers, who swear it's true, the oath of witnesses who say they saw nothing, the few people who *can* see the white flower are mute, because they won't say a word about it to anyone.

Graciela Menéndez, calmly smoothing the edge of the handwoven blanket, you could say it's another way of saying what the Flores brothers are up to, Concha, a fight with the Devil, the people versus terror, and Lucía, of course it is, after what you told us as God intended you to, and bringing out into the open, just like José Matías and Wilber Eduardo, the ghosts that haunt our dreams, it can't be anything else, then Lucía turning to look her in the eyes, and Graciela, despite her strength, a limitless reserve, saucer-sad eyes, an eternity of grayish-black circles under them, Lucía leaning closer, you made that blanket, didn't you Graciela? of course you did, because you do everything so well, and Concepción, satisfied with herself for remembering the anecdote, pleased with herself for mentioning it, content with the fact that she told it, the little old wind-up memory had wound itself up and brought the tale into the light of day, a memory remembering that amongst the *amate* tree's misshapen branches lay a secret, therein an analogical allegory, a fabulous folkloric fable, our *amate* tree, she said, is our hope, our pillar of strength, Concepción, fulfilled, sitting back in her chair, smoking a cigarillo, nearing the end of it, a grayish-blue cloud of smoke distorting the expression on her face, and Lucía, distracted, what's got into my Emiliano? I'm worried, he looked depressed, don't you agree, Concha? but Concepción, turning the pages of another magazine, flipping through it, absorbed in what she was looking at, immersed in the words on the pages, and Graciela, taking Lucía's hand in her own moisturized hand, stroking it, Graciela, the oldest and wisest in the room, *mi querida amiga,* you've got nothing more to worry about than the rest of us, and Concepción, from behind the magazine, that's a lot of comfort to us all, a sarcastic voice that trembled with judgment, insight, appreciation, followed by a discerning squint, and they saw with the eyes of their seasoned understanding, eyes the size of *jacote* or star apples, bringing back their most painful memories, waking up to the truth now and then, and now it was right now, that the world continued to turn round and round with or without them, unfairness fairly dealt with, no correction of the past because you can't change what's wrapped up sewn up at an end polished off, so who is the king of fear and the fearful damage it's done? one king under God, indivisible, with repression and treachery for all, and Graciela Menéndez, poet of the possible, grasping the whole thing, a head on her shoulders that's screwed on right, Graciela repeating, the world goes on turning round and round with or without us, but we can hope and pray, it's all that's left, and since nobody knows and nobody can say why we dream what we dream, our dreams take on the responsibility of having to be dreamt, and in the lapse of time spent in fear, the important thing, *mis amigas,* is for us to keep on praying, relying on them, and keep on hoping, depending on them, pour a little water on them each day to make them grow, as the world continues to turn round and round with or without us, we've still got our hopes and prayers, our dreams, and not some self-deluding fantasy.

Emiliano and Gustavo, returning to the living room together, Gustavo no longer thirsty, Emiliano dragging his feet, a few steps behind Gustavo, leading the way, with a single voice, Emiliano and Gustavo, joined in sorrow, joined in fear, may we come out of this shit in better shape than when we were thrown into it! pronounced with a solemn and heartfelt flavor, a hot tongue scorched and scalded by a double splash of McCormick's Jalisco, Graciela Menéndez looking up at them, a word to the wise is enough, and Graciela, with the Flores brothers' help, and Concepción resting the magazine on her lap to think about it, Lucía twisting herself on the sofa to look at Emiliano and Gustavo, and Concepción, an eye on downcast Emiliano, wait a second, El Puño, she always called him the Fist, you look like death warmed over, and Gustavo, wake up, show us your teeth, what's gotten into you two boys, and Lucía, up from the sofa, reaching for Emiliano, her arm around his shoulders, Leo, sit down here, right beside me, while Gustavo, slumped in a chair, shook his head from side to side, and like lightning his hands were folded, resting in his lap, Graciela making room on the sofa for Emiliano, Gustavo shutting his eyes, a gust of wind rattling the window panes, and Lucía and Emiliano, Gustavo, Concepción, Graciela closing themselves off for a moment from the world accompanied by that feverish wind almost shaking the foundations of Graciela Menéndez's house, until at last, Graciela's boldness, a cocktail of daring, grit and a pair of balls, stepping out from behind the imaginary enclosure raised by the wind, getting up from the sofa, how about some music, *mis amigos?* we can listen through the wound in our hearts.

Jorge Negrete, singer and actor, singing "Paloma querida," as the disc was turning soundlessly, and Graciela Menéndez, swaying with the music, a gentle song, Concepción, putting down her magazine, have you ever seen him in the movies, *mis amigos?* born in Guanajuato, Mexico, a really handsome man, who died when he was forty-two, and Lucía, yes, in *¡Ay Jalisco, no te rajes!* when he met Gloria Marín, Lucía holding Emiliano's hand, a dreamy look in her eyes, he's really something, I can watch him anytime, Concha, and Concepcion, nodding her head at Lucía, then turning in her chair, fixing her eyes on Graciela dancing slowly behind her to the rhythmic *ranchera,* and Concepción, you couldn't have picked a lovelier song, Graciela, to break the spell of fear and dread on behalf of our Flores brothers, and Lucía, that's saying a mouthful Concha, after what Graciela told us, they've got a fight with the Devil ahead of them, and Graciela, coming to a stop where she stood, her arms outstretched, then folded back against her bosom, a gesture to contain herself, security in an uncertain moment, don't mention the Devil, please, not while we're listening to Jorge Negrete, and Graciela, starting up her dance, swaying to the steady pulse of the *ranchera,* ignoring the world and her surroundings, and her friends, to bathe in the warmth of Jorge Negrete's voice, such a novelty it was to wander away from her worries with intrepid shuffling of the feet, wobble, reel and roll, and understated swinging of the hips, wag, shake and twirl, and Hindu-like weaving of the arms, curl, twine and coil, the perpetual dissolving and reforming of the world, and with that allure of attraction, and another song, Lucía taking Emiliano by the hand, rising from the sofa, and Gustavo bowing in front of Concepción, asking for this dance, Concepción flinging the magazine to an empty chair and herself into his arms, Graciela, Lucía and Emiliano, Gustavo and Concepción, together, moving with a smooth wavelike motion in the living room, avoiding the furniture, to another song written by José Alfredo Jiménez, this time a *ranchera valseada,* with the tempo of a waltz, as the disc turned without a sound, Jorge Negrete singing, "La que se fue."

José Matías and Wilber Eduardo, heroic riders traveling in the pickup painted metallic-red but faded into sunburned ecstasy, they weren't like anybody in their right mind, anybody who would've run away without the slightest hesitation from a situation like the one they were facing, a confrontation that was likely going to put them into a tight spot, a new suffering for those who've suffered enough, you can thank your lucky stars, my Flores brothers, and no John Garfield, no Ida Lupino, no Eddie Cantor, no Humphrey Bogart, no Ann Sheridan, no Spike Jones and his City Slickers, *Thank Your Lucky Stars,* 1943, Norman Panama, Melvin Frank, James Kern wrote it, but they've got nothing to do with what José Matías and Wilber Eduardo were going through right now, and no influence on the outcome, they hadn't written that or any other screenplay, so the vulnerable and once-again menaced José Matías and Wilber Eduardo, the Flores brothers, on their way to a destination not far from San Esteban Catarina, to face the Devil, in Graciela's words, but not on their own, with the *cadejos* in the bed of the truck, lying under a tarp in the back next to a case of twelve-ounce cans of Kolashampan Bravo, no barking, no sound at all, the *cadejos,* waiting to do what they could to help the Flores brothers, a pledge of time not money, their task, a kind of vow that was a birthright for all white *cadejos,* magic dogs in the service of José Matías and Wilber Eduardo, who rode in the cab with Graciela Menéndez's talisman between them.

At San Felipe, in Apastepeque, Wilber Eduardo couldn't hold it anymore, he asked his brother to pull off to the side of the road, after they'd gone past the town, and leaving the motor running, doors swung wide open, José Matías joined his brother for a piss over the side of a hill on to the leaves of evergreen shrubs, a yellowthroat rondeletia, a Jewels-of-Opar without Tarzan or Edgar Rice Burroughs nearby, and against the trunks of lofty trees, too, maybe a *huevos de caballo,* the Flores brothers with a view almost due west across the highway, a little more than a mile away, of Cerro Mejía.

There was a rooster crowing, the sun fell artfully toward the horizon, and the Flores brothers, together, a sigh of relief, better to do it now than have to wait, and José Matías, agreeing, and it's nerves, too, that are pushing on my bladder, *mi hermano,* but now it's anticipation, less fear, and we've got the opportunity, the chance we didn't have when they picked us up, beat us to within an inch of our lives, and threw us in the back of a truck, and Wilber Eduardo, buttoning his fly, wiping the dust off his boots against the legs of his trousers, and in a couple of seconds the truck pulled onto CA1W, *Calle Panamericana,* throwing dust into the air from the side of the road.

It won't be long, and we'll have to face it if we can find it, Wilber Eduardo wishing he had a knife or a gun, just in case, and José Matías, reading his mind, it wouldn't do you any good, and you know it, just like a gun wouldn't have got us out of the shit we got into with the National Guard, the National Police, maybe the Treasury Police and ORDEN, and the ride in a helicopter to El Paraíso, fucking Jesus I was scared, José Matías shaking his head, sorry he'd cursed using the name of the Son of God, but it was the magnitude of his fear which he felt like it was yesterday, eating at his soul, grinding his guts, and they turned their eyes to the talisman on the seat between them, looking so small and impotent, a branch cut from a *tihuilote* tree, a young adult after a brief childhood, in the words of Graciela Menéndez, and Wilber Eduardo, just like the way we see ourselves no matter how old we get, like we've never grown up, so how's that branch going to help us bear a lighter burden, how will it help our friends, and the people who suffered that we don't even know? *país mío, tantas veces violado,* country of mine, raped so many times, Wilber Eduardo worrying out loud, and José Matías concentrating on the road, not so far from Laguna Ciega, at a little more than a quarter of a mile in altitude, and in degrees, minutes and seconds, 13°40'60" N and 88°43'60" E, but the distance they were traveling couldn't be measured, not with any numbers, figures, characters, symbols, or units invented until now, José Matías, inventive and respectful contemplation of the Pan-American Highway, CA1W, steering and thinking, his imagination reaching out ahead of them on the way, due regard to most of the written and unwritten rules of the road as the pickup shot past the immutable landscape at high speed on a somewhat uneven highway, eyes straight ahead, but José Matías, now and then, letting his right eye wander, checking on his brother's well-being, right under his brother's nose, without giving himself away, worry was contagious, so he kept his own to himself, overall, getting a lot less worked up than Wilber Eduardo, even now, especially right now, coolheaded on stormy seas, but his knees were jumping, Jose Matías had faith in the talisman, and because he was behind the wheel and couldn't afford the hassle, like an accident that would slow them down, or stop the enterprise in its tracks, he didn't let Wilber Eduardo see a thing, he pressed a free hand down on his trembling knees, not showing his brother more than was necessary, you've got me and that's the end of it, thinking but not saying it, José Matías and Wilber

Eduardo leaving the CA1W and heading north on a curving road toward San Esteban Catarina, the *Calle Panamericana* fading away in the rearview mirror.

Why didn't they put a bullet in us instead? Wilber Eduardo, smoothing his trouser legs, the pickup taking a bump in the road, the creeping underground root of a tree, or a dead animal, and for the Flores brothers it was just a bounce in the front seat of the cab, with a dose of conscience, and the *cadejos,* taking the jolt, it wasn't anything, they weren't really there, invisible to the eye unaided by a supernatural optical instrument, altering the power of vision, it's our imagination again, José Matías gripping the steering wheel, making two not-so-very tight fists, you've got something there, *mi hermano,* they could've used a bullet, two maybe, so we were just lucky, more than 75,000 weren't, fucked up beyond just fucked up, and Wilber Eduardo, gaining strength with anger, José Matías' intention, anger, strength and courage, that's what we need, José Matías saying to himself, and Wilber Eduardo closed his eyes and howled.

At one of the curves before the straightaway they came to San Esteban Catarina, occupying a little more than thirty square miles, nestled on the edge of a mountain at the foot of the *cerro,* Las Delicias, its small population, maybe six thousand inhabitants, dedicated to the cultivation of beans, corn and sugar cane and livestock, but they didn't stop there, at the entrance to the town, they drove slowly into it, at a crawl, taking narrow roads past small stone and brick houses with tiled roofs, climbing a hill, past a long fence made of corrugated iron, folds like a fan, alternate ridges and grooves, palm trees reaching up at the fading sunlight, a boy wearing rubber-soled sandals, orange trousers and a blue and black striped short-sleeved shirt, crouching with his back against a dark blue concrete pillar, a brick wall painted sea blue right behind him, a baby potted palm tree in an old paint bucket stained by white and blue paint, the streets not crowded but busy, life as the sun leaned heavily toward the horizon, a sun-burned man with a deeply lined face wearing a low crown white straw hat and a young man sitting next to him, both of them on a stoop, no sign of danger, no signals charged with menacing currents of electricity, three dogs peering through the bars of an iron fence, here and there a satellite dish on a rooftop, the pickup sluggishly climbing a slight gradient on a low hill, passing a two-story blue and white building on their right, on their left approaching the façade of a pale blue-green church with wide, cream-colored trim and two tall square towers rising on either side with the church's cross in the center between them, placed equidistant from each tower, and José Matías and Wilber Eduardo, on the last leg of their journey, imbued with the courage of their newfound friend, Anastasio Mártir Aquino, *Rey de los Nonualcos,* a symbol of liberation against tyranny, wearing his crown of gold and emeralds, King of the Nonualcos, an indigenous tribe of the Pipil, the Flores brothers, saturated, soaked, bathed in the spirit of Anastasio Aquino, a friendly ghost, *Rey de los Nonualcos*, from Santiago Nonualco, and wise as wise can be, José Matías and Wilber Eduardo, remembering his penultimate words, unspoken but breathed into them, the Flores brothers, Anastasio Aquino pushing the words into them with the force of experience, Those shitty dogs! Kill them! and José Matías and Wilber Eduardo, a loving cavity in their hearts, a cupped hand, protecting those words, never spoken but conveyed by the energy of the King's skillful strategies and past victories, at first an uprising with twenty-five men, catching soldiers of Zacatecoluca regiment unprepared and defeating them, returning to Santiago Nonualco with a lot of weapons and new men that joined his forces along the way, the entire villages of Santiago and San Juan Nonualco, answering his call, as well as Analco, and a part of the town of Zacatecoluca, accompanied by some other villages around the capital, Anastasio Aquino commanding an army of 3000 mostly indigenous men, defeating the official troops sent to San Salvador to conquer the Nonualcos, Anastasio Mártir Aquino, an exemplary fighter and commander of the uprising uniting the claims of villagers, small owners and semi-free laborers in their fight for power against the aristocracy, and when the Flores brothers met him, the three of them drinking *Tic tac,* an *aguardiente,* sitting at a table under the boiling sun, the King of the Nonualcos, neither asleep nor awake, was between this and that, here and there, neither ghost nor flesh and blood, but well placed to give them advice, and now, José Matías and Wilber Eduardo, driving through the streets of San Esteban Catarina, two men and the talisman provided by Graciela Menéndez, her generosity and lasting friendship, a lifelong union, and together, as if the talisman were alive and breathing, the three travelers in the cab of the pickup passed the church on their left, continuing on, José Matías maneuvering the truck, pulling forward, the steering wheel to the left, backing up, the steering wheel to the right, moving forward, reversing, turning around and facing the other direction, pulling over not far from the church and the blue and white painted building with a corrugated iron roof and a sort of awning, an extension of corrugated iron reaching out over the veranda on the ground floor below the roof to protect the entrance from the rain and sun, the school, Complejo Educativo Católico Presbítero Higinio Torres, and José Matías, leaving the engine running, the truck a dozen paces from a turquoise door held open by a rope tied at one end to the handle, the other end to the nearest iron bar in a series of bars in several arched windows without glass, protecting a garage with a silver four-door sedan parked in it.

José Matías lighting a cigarette, a Delta Red from an open pack in his shirt pocket, and Wilber Eduardo, listen closely because you may never hear these words again, can I have a smoke? surprising his brother with the question, Jose Matías, you don't smoke, *mi hermano,* and Wilber Eduardo, I do now, and I did when Graciela told us the story, and José Matías, a true-to-the-spirit sparkle in his eyes, nodding his head, holding the pack in front of his brother, a couple of nervous fingers taking a cigarette out of the crumpled pack, straightening the crooked cigarette before putting it between his lips, waiting for his brother to light it, Wilber Eduardo, filling his lungs, exhaling, I hope it doesn't rain tonight, I like a dark night with a lot of stars, now the sky's glowing amber, and sunset's within reach, a couple of hours to go, maybe less, and Wilber Eduardo, exhaling a lungful, no matter how dark the sky gets tonight, tonight like any other night out here, there'll still be a luminous sea of stars, and you know and I know that cheers me up, *mi hermano,* Wilber Eduardo letting a broad smile cross his face for a couple of seconds before fear that the whole sky would fall down on them, including the talisman they'd promised Graciela they'd return to her in one piece and wrapped in its cloth when they were through, before fear took over and broke his heart, and Wilber Eduardo tossed the butt through the window into the street.

The *cadejos* standing on the pavement outside the truck, having climbed out from beneath the tarp in the back, a little fresh air in the late afternoon, dodging the cigarette butt, listening to the Flores brothers, not having to scratch at fleas, they didn't have fleas, not the magic dogs, the virtuous ones, exemplary, blameless, decent and squeaky clean *cadejos* who existed alongside the evil ones, and José Matías and Wilber Eduardo, sitting quietly in the cab, one brother listening to the other, then José Matías, checking the fuel gauge, turning his head to look his brother in the eyes, it'll be all right, and Wilber Eduardo, *In ixquich nicmati neci yuhquin iztlacapatiliztli — macahmo xinechiztlacahui,* it feels like everything I've ever known was a lie — don't lie to me! and Wilber Eduardo, bowing his head, at once remorseful, wringing his hands, José Matías touching his brother's shoulder, Wilber Eduardo, his mind running, an open faucet, thoughts rushing, saying to himself, it's beside the point, we're at the point of no return, on the horizon the volcano known as Chinchontepec, *Las Chiches,* invincible San Vicente, a stratovolcano, irrelevant, not an elephant, what a ridiculous jump, a thought without reason, this is serious, no joking matter, but levity to levitate by, a kind of music, no elephant and this isn't Sri Lanka and there isn't a circus in town and you aren't in Africa, not Kenya, press your knees together if you've got to piss, or a dance standing in place, maybe hopping from one foot to the other, try it, or just get out of the goddamn truck and take a leak, you're peripheral, on the edge, extraneous, beside the point, so look over there, *pobre infeliz,* it's Chinchontepec, big isn't it, not like you and your brother, small fry, and Wilber Eduardo, his mind telling him nothing, saying everything, nothing good and all bad when you add it up it comes to zero, Wilber Eduardo closing his eyes, and another howl, but it caught in his throat, I need something to drink, looking at his brother, José Matías, who kept on looking straight ahead, feeling everything his brother was feeling, but without breaking out into a sweat, there's a store over there, around the corner, buy us a couple of cold drinks, *mi hermano,* to wet our whistle, and Wilber Eduardo, okay, sure thing, you're right, but I don't want to whistle 'cause I feel like crying, and José Matías, that's the blues you've got hanging 'round your neck, and while you're at it, get me a couple of cigarillos, like the ones Concha smokes, Concepción, a real philosopher, strong as an ox in her temperament, we need all the support we can get, even with this talisman from Graciela's hands, angel hands of Our Lady of the Talisman, Graciela Menéndez, the grateful Flores brothers, José Matías and Wilber Eduardo, about to stand where "death had placed its mark, which weighs like a lead seal at the bottom of a parchment," *Our Lady of the Flowers,* and "in the rain, this black cortège, bespangled with multi-colored faces and blended with the scent of flowers," the nightbird crawled up Wilber Eduardo's sleeve, Wilber Eduardo not bothering to shake it out, it tickled him, I'll keep it there and get out of the truck right now or my thoughts will drive me crazy, and Wilber Eduardo, climbing down from the cab, passing the garage with the silver four-door sedan, disappearing around the corner.

José Matías, sighing, exhausted from sharing the same feelings as his brother, not an observer, an affiliate, the pair of them, bona fide card-carrying members of the same nightmare, and in spite of it, José Matías, keeping a cool head on his shoulders, a double shot of quietude, lighting another cigarette, blowing smoke off to one side, activating the mesolimbic pathway, a real reward system, these Delta Reds, José Matías gawking at a parade in his head, like illustrations in a fairy tale book, a brass band, lords and ladies and the royal retinue, a dozen princesses, all pretty dark girls, and a pale white queen in white lace with a crimson velvet cape around her shoulders, at the tail end the court musicians, guitars and violins, and with each draw on the cigarette, the lords and ladies and a royal retinue, like illustrations in a fairy tale book, marching through a fog of nicotine, lungs and head, the earth didn't shake but he felt as though he'd lost his balance, the lords and ladies and a royal retinue came tumbling downhill, head over heels, bouncing on their way to the rhythm of a daydream, all the colors of pageantry spinning together, a wheel of colors turned behind his eyes, the fluttering wings of angels, We cease being I, and are again this us, *mis amigos,* so don't lose yourselves, return to me, José Matías, attaining a sort of serenity, His Serenity, a title given to a reigning prince, José Matías, a blank man, inhaling deeply, not even thinking, seeing nothing at all, no sunglasses perched on his nose, they were in a case tucked away in the glove compartment, and no need to squint at the sun heading west, no need for anything else, José Matías leaned his head back and shut his eyes.

The main event was ahead of them, José Matías and Wilber Eduardo, they'd do their best, but they weren't Carlos Hernández, "El Famoso," IBF super featherweight champion, "Every time I step into a ring I fight for all of El Salvador," *Saludemos la patria orgullosos, / de hijos suyos podernos llamar,* Let us salute the motherland, / Proud to be called her children, and José Matías, praying right now to have a little of his heart, his guts, Carlos Hernández, a real champion, the Favorite Son, respecting his opponents, never saying a bad word about anyone, adoration, love and respect from his people, José Matías, praying right now with his eyes shut, the Flores brothers had their work cut out for them, vengeance or righteousness? before you weren't cynical, now you are, vengeance is gratifying, but righteousness is like mother's milk, not spilled but sucked right from the nipple, fresh refreshing wholesome-as-nature-meant-it milk, a nation's national pastime coursed in their veins, and love like you've never been hurt, Carlos "El Famoso" Hernández, "There's nothing more satisfying to me than finishing a fight knowing that I invested every last bit of energy in winning, or at least trying to win," the Flores brothers, maybe an echo of the champion's words, a holy guide in their path, a sense of duty compelling them, José Matías, vengeance tastes just right, but righteousness, that's another thing, and Carlos Hernández, "I know that I'm not the most skilled fighter in the world, but nobody can ever claim my heart in the ring," the Flores brothers, a life waiting to happen, an unwavering desire to free the body and soul from hell, wiping the floor with misery, the act of a champion — a man can even see himself — and José Matías and Wilber Eduardo, count them in because they're out, that's what gives them strength, with the help of the talisman, the Flores brothers having taken a pledge, a vow, their aim is true, Wilber Eduardo pulling open the door of the cab, revenge as sweet as *Chocovitos crujientes,* crunchy caramel and chocolate, José Matías opening his eyes, still praying but silently, with the butt of a Delta Red clenched between his teeth, a plastic sack in Wilber Eduardo's hand, a bag long enough to hide the necks of two bottles, the plastic damp with sweat from a pair of ice-cold bottles of beer, José Matías, that didn't take long, and his brother, long enough, you've finished a cigarette, Wilber Eduardo settling himself in the seat, I'd like to smoke one with my beer, *mi hermano,* and José Matías, you've acquired a taste, there's plenty where this one came from, smiling a principled smile but behind the eyes, bitterness and fear, behind the eyes just another totally fucked-over human being, José Matías, like his brother, a man wanting to climb out of the hole somebody else dug for him, a hole they threw him in, covering him with dirt, lying side by side, not literally, telling himself, there's no reason to be scared, damn it, but they'd felt it anyway, the two of them, dead and buried, a herd of heartbeats, a plenitude of panic, nobody ever asking them yes or no, do you accept, don't you accept, do you agree or disagree, but at last, at some point in the ordeal — reflected to perfection by what they'd seen this very morning — a voice telling them, as it told them now, *Macahmo xichoca toyolca cualtiyaz,* stop crying and things will change, and the Flores brothers, hanging on to those words spoken by that voice, a stable surface to cling to in an unreliable, fair-weather world, and still shaking, not so you could see it, but José Matías and Wilber Eduardo, their skin quivering their bones quaking their limbs trembling their bodies convulsing, the Flores brothers, each silent and smoking a cigarette and drinking from a bottle of ice-cold beer in the cab of the truck, the engine switched off, and the sun edging its way toward the horizon.

It was a short distance on foot from where they'd parked the car outside San Esteban Catarina to get to where they were going, approaching now from a different angle than they'd come to it this morning, an auspicious approach, and ten minutes earlier, José Matías and Wilber Eduardo, after finishing a bottle of beer each, the Flores brothers, okay, enough time is being wasted while we wait for the courage to do what we've been intending to do since early today, and José Matías and Wilber Eduardo, the same words came out of their mouths at the same time, José Matías turning the ignition, starting the engine, the truck pulling away from the church of pale blue-green with wide, cream-colored trim and two tall square towers rising on either side with its cross in the center between them, equidistant from each tower, and leaving behind the two-story blue and white school building, Complejo Educativo Católico Presbítero Higinio Torres, the *cadejos* scurrying alongside the truck, all of them passing the town's central park, heading south, the cadejos disappearing and reappearing at different points along the way, and a left turn here, driving past the ironmonger's, a right at the corner of the Farmacia Rivera Damas, the pickup continuing past Farmacia San Esteban and out of town, leaving any trace of life, animal or man, behind them in the rearview mirror, not getting as far as the highway, the *Carretera Panamericana,* the Central American Highway 1, steering the truck off to the side of the road, away from any traffic, parking parallel to cultivated land divided into parcels, shutting off the engine, rolling up the windows, locking the truck, taking the talisman with them and walking, not with long strides but cautiously, using secret threads of communication with the exact spot where they'd seen what frightened them, rising out of nowhere like some ghost or monster in a Mexican horror movie, maybe *El hombre y el monstruo,* or *La muñeca vampira horripilante,* the Flores brothers, side by side, trudging on the earth through the trees and scrub and grass, Las Delicias not far away, rising gently in the near distance, watching them as they gnawed at themselves inside to keep from turning around and going home.

The Flores brothers, José Matías and Wilber Eduardo, taking duty in their stride, Wilber Eduardo, a little Falstaff, reciting a couple of lines: "I am no counterfeit: to die, is to be a counterfeit; for he is but the counterfeit of a man who hath not the life of a man: but to counterfeit dying, when a man thereby liveth, is to be no counterfeit, but the true and perfect image of life indeed — the better part of valor is discretion; in the which better part I have saved my life," and Wilber Eduardo, looking at José Matías, it's another interpretation, my understanding, meaning something else altogether and far from the scholars, more on the order of our being cautious is a lot better than rash courage, yours and mine, *mi hermano,* a little knowledge aforethought, not malice, because being careful, not missing a trick, is the best kind of bravery, and the talisman, a powerful instrument in our hands, Wilber Eduardo, a sort of confidence running through him, and José Matías, putting a hand on his brother's shoulder, Wilber Eduardo's head up, steering toward the wind, as they plowed through the friendly landscape, José Matías reaching for a crushed pack of cigarettes, coming to a halt to light one, cupping his hand to protect the flame from a gust of wind.

As far as they could remember the spot where they'd seen it, the Flores brothers knew they'd recognize the location and that the creature would show itself the way it had shown itself to them in the early part of the day, not known or thought to exist but magnificent in its horror, and the Flores brothers, walking with the same determination as Isabela Corona's single-minded plan of revenge in *El espejo de la bruja,* with a single purpose in mind, and as they were walking, traversing the familiar landscape, by memory as well as instinct, the dapple-gray horse reappeared suddenly in front of them, poking its head around the trunk of a tree not grown anywhere near its full height, Wilber Eduardo grabbing hold of his brother's arm, do you see it? it's the horse again — the magic dogs saw it too — and José Matías stopping in mid-stride, I see it plain as day, *mi hermano,* and it's looking at us, the horse stepping around the tree, standing across the path they were taking, swinging its head around to face them, nodding, moving its head the other way, indicating another path they couldn't see, and the

Flores brothers knowing where they stood and what to expect — something unknown again — and they looked in each other's eyes and each saw what the other was seeing, two brothers and a talisman, José Matías, it's not a time to think about it, and Wilber Eduardo agreeing with his brother, we got this far and there isn't much farther to go, José Matías and Wilber Eduardo, the horse neighing, an animal speaking without saying a word, hurry up or you'll never do it, no sooner are you comfortable with what comes your way than it's over, and something else happens, that's life, and Wilber Eduardo, the horse is right, we were traveling to get the talisman, in safe hands with the task, and worried and nervous and tense on our way back to where we are now, but used to it, and here we find the horse again, and José Matías, or the horse has found us, Wilber Eduardo, so something else has happened, wringing his hands, both of them powerless to change the situation, they didn't move, José Matías, if people talk too much — Wilber Eduardo interrupting him, you've got to be careful about what you say, and the horse was nodding its head, then a gesture from left to right, pointing with its forehead and muzzle in the direction they were supposed to take, José Matías, let's get going, no use in worrying ourselves more than we already have, the Flores brothers, in the same voice, okay, with all the things we want to see, so many, a lot of things to see, we might as well go, and they started walking, following in the horse's hoof steps.

It became so normal, a journey from here to there, the horse taking its time, hoof steps in a lazy slow gait, not far ahead of them, turning its head from time to time to make sure they were following it, the Flores brothers, they could go in any direction, that was called freedom, but they had a specific place in mind, with the horse as a guide, something to do that couldn't be avoided, not at any cost, José Matías and Wilber Eduardo, committed to erasing something that didn't have a right to exist, not anymore, it was their turn, and José Matías and Wilber Eduardo, a daytime dream of ruling, an ambition that was good for the health, because anger rose in their guts from time to time, and it had to go somewhere, rockets in unison launched by the Flores brothers: we'll wipe the fucking thing off the face of the earth, an ambition cultivated by the suffering of a thousand years ago, it was that far away, but they couldn't help remembering it, each day a minute's silence, how many it's-too-lates given with a tormented face, this is a hard life we suffer, voices all around them, Wilber Eduardo and José Matías, on that day we all died, one way or another, until now, because it's not too late, and the magic dogs, almost nipping at their heels, we'd better stick around and watch out for the Flores brothers, it's been a long day, the *cadejos,* loyal, and not to be seen by José Matías and Wilber Eduardo until the right moment.

The landscape wasn't in their imaginations, neither of the Flores brothers was dreaming beyond the momentary dream of revenge, a luxury of adrenaline, the horse leading the way, a path they didn't remember, but they hadn't approached the place where they were frightened from the same direction as they were approaching it now, and the march was brought to a halt before time, the horse turning to face them, a couple of words, a bit of advice from the horse's mouth, a dapple-gray horse going down on its knees, first the forearms then the knees, for a kind of whisper, a confidence, one horse to two men, a willing accomplice or a herald bringing news from a distant world, without the wings of an angel, but a pat on the back from a comrade, the *cadejos* taking a breather, the Flores brothers watching, the horse's lips didn't move, it wasn't *Mister Ed,* from 1961, not just a word but a recitation, a quote from the beginning of *El espejo de la bruja,* they were hearing it but didn't believe it, how did the horse know they'd been thinking of *El espejo de la bruja,* wonder of wonders is the world of animals and man, and José Matías and Wilber Eduardo, sitting down Indian style to listen, cross-legged, folding their hands, Wilber Eduardo holding the talisman in his lap, and the horse, not speaking out loud, pronouncing each word with well-earned importance, "Since the dawn of civilization until today, witchcraft and magic have existed, as well as its practitioners, magicians, sorcerers and witches. This mysterious caste, in which women are among the most devoted, includes those initiated in the boundless field of secret knowledge known as Arcane Sciences or Occultism. They are guilty of many crimes and hideous practices. They blaspheme, they sacrifice unchristened children, they swear in the name of Satan, they kill people and have them cooked, they feed on carrion and hanged men's corpses, they kill with poisons and spells, they cause madness, and hundreds of other horrors that riddle the history of this damned caste. To use their diabolical powers, witches resort to special potions, brooms, skeletons of children and animals, every kind of untanned hide, flasks and vessels of every shape, secret powders and dreadful poisons, and an infinite variety of lethal herbs. All this is used by an average witch. But only a superlative witch, endowed with genuinely profound knowledge of the occult, can make use of a magical object of infinite powers and properties invented by a great magician of ancient Persia. The mirror."

The dapple-gray horse taking air into its lungs, moving its prehensile lips, baring its sturdy teeth like dominoes, exhaling through its nostrils, breaking off long enough to breathe, at last a few more words, a tip-off, beware of the presence of a mirror, and the horse shaking its head, mane and forelock sending motes of dust flying in the failing sunlight, the equine eye the largest of any land mammal, not perfectly spherical, flattened anterior to posterior, hazel eyes watching them, and José Matías and Wilber Eduardo, a single drawn-out sigh between them, the horse got slowly to its feet, turning away, continuing along the path it was leading them on, the Flores brothers following suit, without exchanging a glance, nothing surprised them anymore, they'd been forewarned, but they didn't have any memory of a mirror that went along with the frightening thing they'd seen in the early part of the day; I think we must've dreamed what we heard, *mi hermano,* and José Matías, brushing the dirt off the back of his trousers, since when can horses talk, and without moving its lips like some kind of ventriloquist, but the words they'd heard, because the Flores brothers did hear them regardless of where they came from, inside or outside, added an ounce of fear to the ingredients of the recipe they'd put together for a savory dish of revenge meant to purify, cleanse and unburden them, something they hadn't expected at this particular moment, on their way to settle the affair, convinced that the talisman would do the job no matter what they faced, José Matías and Wilber Eduardo, uncertainty, not thinking anything of it until now, feeling that the drowsiness of death would soon be lifted from them, not taking into account their own danger, the Flores brothers, walking silently behind the horse, death always ends by imposing silence on those who contemplate it, because that's what they were thinking, maybe they wouldn't get out of it alive, it was a hideous monster, with the appearance of something they'd surely seen in a Mexican horror movie, *El hombre y el monstruo, El barón del terror,* and now the possibility of something straight out of *El espejo de la bruja,* no end to the lengths their minds wandered in the dark as their feet took them to the place where they'd been so frightened, José Matías and Wilber Eduardo, a threat to their daytime dream of ruling that had to be shrugged off, the dapple gray slowing down, the Flores brothers catching up, a brother walking on either side of the horse, stroking its flank, reaching for its withers, the dapple gray nodding, accepting the tenderness, wanting to offer something in return, more than the cautionary words it'd given them, without moving its lips, no *Mister Ed,* and the Flores brothers, what a beautiful horse, what fine features, our dapple gray deserves a portrait painter from the seventeenth century, *mi hermano,* and Wilber Eduardo, your words for this creature are a beacon in the stormy sea, José Matías looking brighter, the world looking brighter, a bright future, José Matías, a little more of our scarce resources are needed to succeed, to rid the place of an evil spirit, not to mention we've got the talisman, and Wilber Eduardo, the sun isn't cooking us in its vapor, the horse nudging him gently, saying go on, so Wilber Eduardo, we'll do this with the joy it deserves, and the halting dapple gray, waiting now until they were ahead of him, the Flores brothers listening, the horse's lips didn't move, but a voice they heard, they'd turned to face it, you're worthy to be involved in this, both of you, on behalf of everyone you know, and everyone you don't know — and that's plenty, the dapple gray moving its lips, without baring its teeth, a few more gentle words of encouragement, you're innocent before God and before men, and the Flores brothers, together, in a single voice, it's a matter of honor, the horse walking ahead of them, José Matías and Wilber Eduardo, more convinced than ever of their obligation to the task, on a merciful march, striding confidently behind the horse, long decisive steps in a specified direction, but they weren't fools, and they proceeded with caution.

All of life and its possibilities, from this point on, lay ahead of them, José Matías and Wilber Eduardo, the landscape and their future rolling out like a long, narrow rug or a strip of carpet, their destination in sight, and now, *Siento como si todo lo que haya conocido fuera mentira,* I feel as though everything I've ever known was a lie, didn't mean as much to them as it'd meant a little while ago, not in Náhuatl, the language of the Aztecs, not in Spanish, and the Flores brothers, their heads together, standing still behind the dapple gray, who'd kept on walking until it disappeared between a couple of strong and leafy *tempisque* trees, José Matías, let's see the talisman, *mi hermano,* the branch of the *tihuilote* tree that had risen from the floor of Blanca's two-room shack, Blanca giving the talisman to Graciela Menéndez, here, *m'hija,* take it, the branch of this *tihuilote* tree with its flowers and fruit, leaves that will stay green and live forever, it's your souvenir, and it will keep you from harm, you won't lose your tenderness, it's your talisman — don't be surprised, I know what you're thinking — it will love you and defend you to the death, like a sister, Graciela Menéndez letting the Flores brothers borrow it, Wilber Eduardo, unwrapping the talisman, a cloth made of a very soft material, protecting it from all kinds of weather and temperatures, water, dirt and dust, the same cloth Blanca gave Graciela after reaching into her heavy-looking trunk, digging around in it, a bottomless trunk, Blanca saying, always keep it wrapped in this, and now the talisman in the Flores brothers' hands, an evolving, dawning talisman, budding like the compact, knoblike growths on the *tihuilote* tree, already developed into flowers, blossoming right in front of Graciela's eyes, and Wilber Eduardo, standing next to a giant *amate* or it could've been a tall *jocote* tree, his tenderness for the same flowers that had blossomed right in front of Graciela's eyes, and the green leaves, José Matías and Wilber Eduardo, together, feeling someone or something looking at them, a nearby *Tabebuia rosea,* the maquilishuat tree, the Flores brothers looked up at it — speaking of flowers and speaking of eyes — a few large funnel-shaped purple flowers with yellow eyes fading to white, eyes squinting at them without blinking, appreciating the beauty of the talisman in their hands, funnel-shaped flowers, almost showing a smile if they'd had a mouth and lips, and Wilber Eduardo, but flowers can't smile, can they, José Matías grinning at him, a little foolish at a time like this, but Wilber Eduardo, composed and poised, reciting part of a poem:

All have come
from where the flowers arise.
The flowers that confuse the people,
which cause their hearts to whirl.
They have come to scatter,
to make them fall like in a rain,
garlands of flowers,
intoxicating flowers.

And José Matías, looking at his brother with admiration, putting him on a pedestal, José Matías saying, reciting Alfonso Quijada Urías, a little Falstaff, and now Xayacamach! a poet, a composer of songs — with thanks to León-Portilla — but Xayacamach, that's really something, you knock me out, what you know could fill a thousand barrels, *mi hermano,* I really mean it, Xayacamach, born around the middle of the fifteenth century, a legend then, a few words now, and the lord of Huexotzinco, Tecayehuatzin, the lord of Huexotzinco liked him a lot, valued him, and I quote, "so highly that he included him among those few he chose to converse with on the meaning of 'flower and song,'" it's not for nothing he held him in high esteem, of course, and José Matías, taking a breath of air, a lot of talking, maybe a dry throat, José Matías reaching out, touching his brother's face with the palm of his hand, I've got a lot of respect for you, too, *mi hermano,* higher than high, and Wilber Eduardo caressing his brother's face in return, the Flores brothers, without thinking, on their way again, not tiptoeing, but careful just the same, and while they were walking, José Matías, clearing his throat, he had more to say, a light in his eyes lit by the lamp of love, José Matías, those flowers in the poem by

Xayacamach — the composers of songs talked about them together with the lord of Huexotzinco, poets gathered round the lord of Huexotzinco, and I quote again, "discussing the ultimate meaning of 'flower and song,' poetry, and the universe of the symbols" — the words you just recited, Xayacamach's words, maybe he's comparing those flowers to hallucinogenic mushrooms? to *teonanácatl?* taking us to a faraway world? what do you think, *mi hermano?* and Wilber Eduardo, a smile warmed by mutual brotherly love, a worthy head held high, I can't think for you, but we think alike, it would explain a lot of things, wouldn't it, hallucinogenic mushrooms, maybe they are, maybe they aren't, we can ask ourselves another question, in the same vein, is all of this happening for real? what difference does it make? but one thing's for sure, we haven't swallowed psilocybin, and we aren't in a dream world, we're where we are right now with the talisman and a mission in front of us, the Flores brothers, not looking where they were going, their eyes fixed on each other, lost in conversation, the trees and plants and the sky itself watching them, José Matías and Wilber Eduardo, almost tripping and falling over a few rocks in their path — where did those come from? — stumbling, grabbing hold of each other to steady themselves, remaining upright, then looking up from the ground on which they were standing and recognizing the exact spot where they'd seen a ghost or monster straight out of a Mexican horror movie, and their fate was upon them, right there before their eyes.

On the journey from here to there and there to here, José Matías and Wilber Eduardo, dragging the unwanted past with them, imposed on the Flores brothers, and Wilber

Eduardo, is all of this happening for real? no *teonanácatl,* no hallucinogenic mushrooms taking us to a faraway world, but there's a reason for everything, and if you buy that there's a bridge for sale, because "people will buy anything that's 'one to a customer,'" and the ghost or monster, a face out of a Mexican horror movie, maybe *El hombre y el monstruo* was more like it, as real as the sun crawling toward the horizon, or a gust of dry wind, but who or what was it that was transformed into a menacing face, Wilber Eduardo, the world seems lonely and large, and trees figuring in every part of it, let's count them: the story of Graciela Menéndez and Blanca the witch, the talisman, the *tihuilote* tree, the big balsam — *bálsamo del Perú* — and its vanilla-scented resin, *tempisque* trees, an *amate,* maybe a White Sapote, known as *cochitzapotl,* and a shady tree called *Yaxché,* the ceiba tree, and the maquilishuat tree, its purple flowers with yellow eyes fading to white watching them right now, flowers swiveling to see their own surroundings, and in particular, keeping an eye on José Matías and Wilber Eduardo, flowers swiveling through an angle of approximately 270°, moving like an owl's head, the Flores brothers, never out of nature's sight, in the surrounding landscape, low and high grass, dried and washed-out yellow or almost luscious green, immaculate parcels of cultivated land, and the eyes of the flowers of the *Tabebuia rosea* burning holes in the back of their heads, José Matías and Wilber Eduardo approaching an indistinct shape, obscure and inexplicable, a few feet away, with a sort of multifaceted head, a bit like the compound eye of an insect, a head on shoulders of an ever-changing form, a mutable body with self-contradictory elements, maybe gaseous, the Flores brothers, in the same voice at the same time, what the fuck is it? they were standing closer to it and staying long enough in one place to observe the same thing they'd seen for only a moment earlier in the day, a head with five faces, like all the fingers of one hand — fingers or faces, who needs more than six to put the fear of God into him — a head with the faces of dangerous men, let's make a list, here's a name or two, take your pick, maybe General Reyes Vehemente or General José Enrique Embustera, defense minister at the time of "Operación Rescate," guardians of order, or Second Lieutenant Daniel Sánchez, commander of a unit in the Las Hojas massacre, or Major Inocente Fumier, who gave the order to assassinate Archbishop Romero, or Captain Ángel Echeverría, involved in the killing, or Captain Oscar Napoleón Rodríguez, *El Carnicero de El Junquillo,* notorious in Morazán, or Lieutenant Colonel Dionisio López Morales, commander of *Batallón Ramón Belloso* during the massacre in and around El Mozote, or a soldier, a member of the *Batallón Atlacatl,* who'd drawn a chalk skull in the confessional of a church in El Mozote, with the words "Atlacatl Battalion. Hell's angels," exactly which faces didn't matter, don't bother counting them, and the words of Archbishop Romero, "Let there not be so many crimes and abuses with impunity and, even though they may wear military uniforms, they must face justice and give an accounting for what they have done and to receive appropriate punishment if it has to do with common crimes," enemies' faces gathered together — plenty of faces to choose from — and a body that was almost solid, a cloud growing denser by the second, taking on a familiar shape, a vision making their slicked-back hair stand on end, a little Vaseline and Brylcreem, José Matías and Wilber

Eduardo, and a reminder of what once was and yet could be, a real threat to life and limb, a body large and wavering like the wobbly rising heat from the highway in oppressive sunlight, branches that were arms with shoots like fingers, not suckers springing from the main stock, a treelike shape, a manlike shape, vapor or gas, a fuel, flammable? — the *cadejos* fearlessly scampering between the slender trunks of half-grown trees with the spirit of puppies — the Flores brothers, witnesses, like nothing they'd ever seen before it had shown itself to them in the early part of the day, not known or thought to exist but magnificent in its horror.

Wilber Eduardo almost dropping the talisman, their limbs shaking, fingers trembling, and José Matías, right beside him, patting his shirt pocket, searching without looking for a crushed pack of Delta Reds, not letting his eyes turn away from the thing, and at all times, at the most unexpected moments, José Matías sizing up the situation, remembering what had happened and when, a lifetime ago, like a distant hello, kicked and beaten and thrown into a truck, a helicopter ride, it was just the beginning of it, a metal bed-frame, a sort of *parrilla,* and a bucket of water as big as a tub, tortured, hearing the national anthem everyday at 6:00 a.m., a burned corpse stinking like burned roast pork wrapped in a plastic sheet, not the only corpse, more like a dozen under the same roof, and there were plenty more they didn't see, José Matías, speaking out loud, the truth that words reflect in their silence frightens the lieutenants, captains, colonels, generals, Treasury Police, National Police, National Guard, ORDEN, *uno, dos, tres, cuatro, cinco y seis,* all the way to the top, who's the President, I'm the President, the lot of them, you can't count them on one hand, not even two, you'd need dozens, hundreds, maybe thousands, nobody's got that many hands — no fucking branches or arms with shoots like fingers — and you can't pay them back because there isn't enough of that kind of money, so you can't get even or even the score — owing to the fact that I'm nervous, not even doing a slow burn, I'm repeating myself, maybe I'm cracking up — but this much I know and it's more than enough, "what frightens them is the truth that words reflect in their silence," if you get my drift, *mi hermano,* of course you do, I'm preaching to the choir, but fuck it! words put across what everybody likes better not to say, mostly people who prefer silence, lies, conformity, for example — I'm really putting two and two together — those soldiers, lieutenants, captains, colonels, generals, Treasury Police, National Police, National Guard, ORDEN, *chingaban a la gente común y corriente como vos y yo,* they fucked up people like you and me, the average joe, fucked forever, and José Matías, fidgeting with the thoughts in his head, he couldn't keep them to himself, they were pouring out all over him, tick tick tick, and bang! like he'd lost it, trying to light a cigarette without watching the match blown out by a breeze or the steaming breath of the thing jumping around like a flame in front of them, José Matías, the sentences kept on tumbling out of his mouth, landing at his brother's feet, you can't even count them on a hundred thousand hands, to say nothing of the faces on the head in front of us, this I-don't-know-what, a motherfucker, that's what, this thing scaring the shit out of us again, maybe an airlike fluid substance expanding freely to fill any space available, or a gaseous substance suspended in the air, normally liquid — but hang on a minute, *mi hermano,* you've got to help me get this cigarette lit.

Wilber Eduardo, cupping his free hand around the flame, thinking out loud, maybe it's panic, what he's saying, a mouthful, my panic-struck brother, but it isn't the time for us to panic, so many saints might've panicked in our lifetime, so many saints crushed under the heel, the rim of the horn-rimmed glasses ground into dust, I thought it'd be me jumping out of my skin, what the hell, but you never know, a level head at a time like this! Wilber Eduardo, a calm step back now that the cigarette was burning, his brother taking a hard pull on it, almost smoking the whole thing down in a breath, and Wilber Eduardo, we've landed right in the middle of what happened to us when we were twenty-five, José Matías, in the middle of shit, more than thirty years ago, a thousand years ago, it was that far away, a lifetime, but right now, wind your watch and check the time, it's you and me with a job to do, and Wilber Eduardo shook his brother gently but firmly by the shoulders without dropping the talisman.

The Flores brothers turning to look at the thing in front of them, it'd changed while Wilber Eduardo was busy shielding a flame for his brother's cigarette, what now? a single face with a combination of features of people they knew or had known, people tortured or killed, including Elio, Wilber Eduardo's childhood friend, a young man with the same nickname as Mama Lola's son Rogelio, the Flores brothers, hey, there's Elio's nose before it was broken, or the familiar look in a pair of his wandering eyes before they were black and blue — it was no accident, a rifle butt on the side of the head, a fist landing a punch that broke Elio's nose, which came first they didn't know — remember? a photograph of his body pinned to a wall, a National Guard souvenir, but what's a picture of Elio doing here, and Wilber Eduardo, at the time, recognizing Elio through his own bruised black eye, the two of them black-eyed friends, one in this life, one in the next, and the Flores brothers in the right-this-minute bad dream, the eternalness of their love, scrutinizing the monster's face, finding a feature belonging to Benavides, fucked up by the National Guard, his ears on the monster's face, or maybe his eyebrows — Benavides, a little simpleminded on account of brain damage, a suffering that lasts — and there, maybe pointing, there's Rosita's hair, long, dark and thick, a heartache to see parts of the faces of their friends on this monster, Rosita, who'd said: if I hadn't ducked so fast a bullet would've split my head in two, but later the same day another bullet, hitting her this time, a bull's eye, ripping through the skull, her shiny skin sweating under the hot sun, parting her hair, parting her skull, and *cariño,* that's what she used to whisper to José Matías, they were fourteen, and later, too, teenagers, maybe seventeen if they were a day, *cariño,* my dear, or *cielo,* always a sweet word for José Matías, and when José Matías heard the story, Luis Hernández telling him what he'd seen in Morazán — how the fuck did she get to Morazán? — it was like José Matías was seeing it happen with his own eyes, José Matías listening, taking it in but hard to believe, there were plenty of tears, a real shame, a tragedy, one more tragedy, and Wilber Eduardo holding his brother in his arms, trying to comfort him, Luis Hernández, standing there helpless, I'm sorry I'm sorry I'm sorry, I had to tell you, but she shouldn't have been there in the first place, not exactly there, she was offering us a little help, the battle line, the supplies used up, the food gone, the ammunition stores almost depleted, our Rosita, she'd been helping women, children, and old people to get to Villa El Rosario and the church, and wham!—right on target, before she got them anywhere, dead as a doornail, and the Flores brothers, especially José Matías right now, a condition like shock seeing Rosita's waist-length black hair on a monster out of a Mexican horror movie, a monster whose face was made up of bits and pieces, wrinkles and creases of people they knew or had known, Wilber Eduardo, this has got to stop, and José Matías, a man in one piece after a cold sweat, I'm with you, *mi hermano,* now and forever, and Wilber Eduardo, down on one knee, unwrapping the talisman in front of the monster like an airlike fluid substance expanding freely to fill the space in front of them, and it was a lot of space, the outdoors, and José Matías agreeing with his brother, the world is lonely and large.

In the meantime, the gaseous cloud, a river at floodtide flowing in reverse, growing less dense by the second, blurry and quivering like a flame, and the Flores brothers, we've seen this before, not bearing the facial features of anyone they knew or had known, not anymore, something isn't right, no monster out of a Mexican horror movie, it was a trick, a lure, in bad taste, an invitation on top of a glimmering transparent thing, Monsignor Romero's face, a distorted face, and then his body appearing out of the quivering flame, a body twisted in pain, his heart bleeding from a bullet, Wilber Eduardo, an index finger pointing, there's the stain, shot while elevating the chalice at the end of the Eucharistic rite, celebrating mass in the Chapel of the *Hospital de la Divina Providencia,* and José Matías, hurriedly helping his brother unwrap the talisman, the Flores brothers, their heads down, a murmuring voice, and Wilber Eduardo, I can't hear him, what's he saying? the Flores brothers hearing it, "Who knows if the one whose hands are bloodied with Father Grande's murder, or the one who shot Father Navarro, if those who have killed, who have tortured, who have done so much evil, are listening to me? Listen, there in your criminal hideout, perhaps already repentant, you too are called to forgiveness," Óscar Arnulfo Romero y Galdámez, murdered by right-wing assassins, a single shot in the heart, and José Matías, what day is it? maybe *Jornada de Solidaridad Continental Monseñor Romero,* looking at his wristwatch as if he could concentrate to read the date on the dial, almost forgetting what he was doing, Wilber Eduardo, fumbling with the cloth covering the talisman, what sort of face is it now? — this business of constantly changing its appearance is driving me nuts, perpetrator to victim and back again — the Flores brothers not daring to look at it, but José Matías, seduced by curiosity, unable to resist a quick glance, shutting his eyes almost immediately, Holy Mother of God, don't look now, *mi hermano,* you won't like what you see, it isn't a Divine Countenance, José Matías mumbling, better dead better dead, and Wilber Eduardo, knock it off, so many doubts, emotions, reactions, but a head bearing their own two faces, José Matías' and Wilber Eduardo's, the Flores brothers, and a third, too, but unidentifiable.

The Flores brothers with the talisman in their hands, the soft cloth that covered it lying on the ground, José Matías and Wilber Eduardo, now you see it now you don't, facing their own likenesses on the monster's head floating above a gaseous shape their own height, three faces gathered together, a sort of tricorne sitting on a reeking ethereal body the width of outspread arms, not a strand of Rosita's hair or a thread of the Monsignor's violet clerical skullcap, a *paonazza* zucchetto, the third face the property of a burned corpse, anonymous or the same one they'd seen wrapped in plastic, without features, but now, together with their own faces, Wilber Eduardo, I'm going to be sick, it's too much, and José Matías, everything we've been through until now has been too much, if you add it up, *mi hermano,* now's our chance, an opportunity that's a gift from Graciela Menéndez and Blanca, and Wilber Eduardo, so we've got no choice, José Matías, the thing we see now is what I remember seeing earlier today, Wilber Eduardo, there's no way to kill it, and I'm not sure I want to, it isn't a matter of them or us, it's us, our faces, our suffering, a symbol of souls in torment, José Matías' arms holding him until he let go of his fear, and Monsignor Romero's words ringing in their ears, "The cry of liberation of our people is a clamor that rises up to God and that no one or nothing will be able to stop now," José Matías, we've got to release ourselves and the burned corpse — why we're paired with it I don't know — from what holds us back, memory and hardship itself, we've got to help our souls along on their trip to the other world, even if we aren't dead yet, and Wilber Eduardo, since we aren't dead yet, we must be seeing our deaths to come, what's real and what isn't doesn't mean a thing anymore, not like it used to when we were innocent, José Matías, we were kids then, *mi hermano,* and we won't have to kill it, it'd be like killing ourselves, and Wilber Eduardo, there's nothing as moving as a man using the gift God's given him, let's get to work.

The Flores brothers, together, moving forward with caution, approaching the monster, it wasn't a movie, and into the bargain, growing branches like arms and sprouts like fingers, not flailing branches and pointing sprouts with leaves but outstretched arms and grasping fingers, who'll get there first, those branches and sprouts like fingers or us? Wilber Eduardo talking to the air, and the Flores brothers, staring themselves in the face, and a third face reduced to carbon, a tricorne that made their heads spin, José Matías whispering, but it didn't look anything like a tree the first time we saw it, Wilber Eduardo, by magic it's turned into something compatible with our talisman, the Flores brothers considering the potency of the *tihuilote* tree from Graciela's story, Blanca turning her head toward Graciela, how about a *tihuilote* tree, *jovencita*? and I'll make it come right out of the floor, you'll like that, won't you? it'll be the first time, something new, and a story to tell your children, and the Flores brothers, together, it's as close to a *tihuilote* tree as a thing like that could be, the talisman already at work with a power greater than they could've imagined, José Matías and Wilber Eduardo, a human being's limited creative power, a brain knocked off its axis more than thirty years ago, the Flores brothers would get rid of it, wipe the slate clean, make the past go away, erase this thing made of who-knows-what that'd suddenly turned into a sort of tree, Wilber Eduardo, click, a thought, now the branch will fit it like a key in a lock, José Matías, it's the most beautiful thing in the world — the public rose to applaud them, to keep their spirits up — and a simple formula handed to us by Our Savior the Branch of a *tihuilote* tree, without an effort on our part, apart from courage, José Matías and Wilber Eduardo recognizing the opportunity from Graciela's words, the significance of the talisman, the Flores brothers, in a single voice, a sort of supernatural tincture I can taste on the tip of my tongue, freshly laundered, then or now it doesn't make a difference, we're outside the circle of time, people only a dream, at least for as long as we fight the good fight, with no interruptions, and the Flores brothers, in the knowledge that words alone weren't enough, advancing until they were right in front of it, frightened and resolute, ready to vomit and unshakable, a sigh like a whisper from far away, without hearing it, with sustenance, reassurance, encouragement, maybe Graciela Menéndez, Emiliano, El Puño, Concepción, Concha — she always called him the Fist — Lucía, Gustavo, Benavides, Alfonso and Margó, a sigh that included a population they couldn't see but felt from the groin down to their feet, succor for their aching hearts.

José Matías and Wilber Eduardo, tickled by the leaves of a branch reaching out to them with sprouts growing hastily, the magic metamorphosis was in a hurry, tickling like feathers, they wouldn't step back, the Flores brothers wanting to laugh but keeping themselves ready, an undertaking, a maneuver, initiative and measures, an operation the Flores brothers were about to begin — are there methods that'll give us the shove to direct our thoughts in such a way that we'll put in motion something to achieve the results we're looking for? — and a voice saying, don't think about it, boys, here's the talisman, there's the place on the tree where the branch belongs, just connect the dots, or in this case, plug her in, step back, and let her go! vroom! too much thinking spoils the whole escapade, it's not illegal under the law, but if it were we'd make our own laws, isn't that right, boys? the Flores brothers nodding their heads, and in a single voice, we've got two lives and one address, and those are words of wisdom, so thank you, whoever you are, and José Matías, a grin as wide as his skin would stretch, and Wilber Eduardo, joy to the new-found King — what time of year is it anyway? 'cause that isn't the phrase, it's something about glory, but the pages are blank blank blank, the Flores brothers, their minds with nothing in them, that's how we operate, easier done than said or thought about too long, it's action that counts, the contents aren't illegal because there aren't any, blank blank blank, we're predicting a muta-tion, a conversion, a complete reorganization, and truly looking forward to the destruction of a monster — not a monster out of a Mexican horror movie, more like a mani-festation of our fears, the hole of suffering we're standing in that we never dug ourselves and haven't been able to climb out of until now, with Charlie Poole's version of a song by Rufe K. Stanley, "Where The Whippoorwill Is Whispering Goodnight."

> *By the fireside one familiar face is missing*
> *That tender smile no longer greets my sight*
> *In that quaint old-fashioned home tonight I'm listening*
> *Where the whippoorwill is whispering goodnight.*

The thing, now fully transformed into a *tihuilote* tree ready for the Flores brothers to fit the magic branch in place, stood there looking at them, José Matías and Wilber Eduardo star-ing back at their own faces, a revolving tricorne, averting their eyes from the face reduced to carbon, a wretched vi-sion, too odious to look at, the *cadejos* waiting in case there was an attack, and Graciela Menéndez from somewhere far away, Our Savior the Flores Brothers, and Emiliano,

Concepción, Lucía, Gustavo, Benavides, maybe Alfonso and Margó, repeating after her, a sort of call and response, Our Savior the Flores Brothers, then all together, voices climbing to the heavens — a vault where the sun, moon, stars and planets are located, check your celestial charts — Graciela, Emiliano, Concepción, Lucía, Gustavo, Benavides, maybe Alfonso and Margó, compatible voices saying with exuberance as if they were singing it, the sun rose with explosions in the sky, animals, plants and trees tickled pink, dusty trails, worn paths and long highways on cloud nine, rivers, ravines and volcanoes on top of the world — that's right, "Made it, Ma! Top of the world!" — and Graciela, dancing whirling howling, all of them, together, no holding hands, it doesn't work like that, but Graciela Menéndez, Emiliano, Concepción, Lucía, Gustavo, Benavides, maybe Alfonso and Margó, shouting out loud: do it do it do it, fit the magic branch of the *tihuilote* tree where the tree needs a branch, plug it in, our Flores brothers, put that key in the lock and turn it, seal it up, for the love of God! and watch our enemies turn to stone, all the while the Flores brothers hearing nothing, concentration as sharp as a razor's edge, and Wilber Eduardo, ready with a quote from W. Somerset Maugham, "The dead look so terribly dead when they're dead," they were trying to shake off the effect of seeing their own faces in front of them, joined with another, a face burned to a crisp, on the shoulders of a *tihuilote* tree, and José Matías and Wilber Eduardo each taking hold of the magic branch Graciela Menéndez had given them, José Matías' right hand, Wilber Eduardo's left, bringing the branch closer to where it belonged on the tree's sturdy trunk, right there, you see, it's as plain as the nose on your face, the tree with their faces on it, not wavering like a flame, but standing there with roots reaching deep into the ground, and a long, drawn-out gust of wind whistling through branches of nearby trees and shrubs as the sun met the horizon, dropped off the edge of the earth and left a glow like reddish-orange fire in the sky.

Who sings the loudest and the longest, happiness or pain? The exhilaration the Flores brothers would soon share with all the others who knew and felt that, at this very moment, they were doing away with their past, the monster from a Mexican horror movie, or an ever-present insufferable suffering capable of singing its lousy song until the end of all days, their exhilaration was waiting at the doorstep, reach down and pick it up, but now, José Matías and Wilber Eduardo, with the talisman in their hands, facing the world, a world endlessly creating new wretchedness and death, a machine that didn't even stop for lunch in its production of misery, a world that kept on turning, don't trip over the spinning ball, José Matías, looking his brother in the eyes, we can't stop now, *mi hermano,* just because suffering lives on everywhere else in the world, and Wilber Eduardo, of course not, and we can't forget the daring it took to get us here, the Flores brothers moving forward, inching the branch into place, a spot created for it by the magic of the talisman, not having to screw it in, it just fit where it went, right where it was meant to be, José Matías and Wilber Eduardo, singing a saying to unhappiness, "I can do all things through him who strengthens me," straight from the

English Standard Version, a faith that shook a nearby volcano, and when the talisman, a branch from the *tihuilote* tree, found its place among other branches of this *tihuilote* tree, anchored in place — a man among men, a woman among women — the Flores brothers, we've done it! a voice they shared with the same force at the same moment, it's done, stepping back from the tree, feeling the heat emanating from it, without warning a combustible substance, organic but otherworldly, a temperature bordering on the impossible, the *cadejos* right behind them, don't get too close, José Matías and Wilber Eduardo, another couple of steps away from the tree, not turning their backs on it, a formidable foe, José Matías, don't blink, *mi hermano,* because in the twinkling of an eye it might just reach out and grab us, the Flores brothers, facing an uncomfortable situation, yet all they had to do was attach the branch to the *tihuilote* tree, and they'd done it, it was done, following a hunch they didn't have until the last minute, Graciela Menéndez didn't give them a handbook when she gave them the talisman, nothing said, nobody told them what to do, but their intuition, almost an instinct, and now another couple of steps back, moving behind a mango tree, it could've been an *amate,* or a gumbo-limbo, the *chaká,* known as *sip' che'* in Mayan, whose nectar is the antidote to the poison of the *chechen,* the black poisonwood tree — wherever the *chaká* is found, the *chechen* is near — and the Flores brothers, they were behind a mango tree, protecting themselves from the high temperature of the *tihuilote,* where's all that heat coming from? peeking around the trunk of the mango, they hadn't burned incense, nor sprinkled the *tihuilote* with a single petal of a flower, nor spilled a drop of alcohol made from sugarcane to help the souls along on their trip to the other world, once and for all, for José Matías and Wilber Eduardo, a ceremony of weightless love, and wings, and they hadn't circled around the tree three full turns to the right, nor four turns to the left, to confuse the souls so they couldn't return to this "life of poverty and suffering," like a real burial, Wilber Eduardo, but maybe that's only in Guatemala, in the words of Arias, anyway, it doesn't matter, but what did matter was the victory, and the enthusiasm won by the long-standing urge to do something for themselves, and for others, the *tihuilote* tree with three faces, José Matías' and Wilber Eduardo's, and an anonymous face, burned beyond recognition, I can't stand to look at it, the whole thing generating unbearable heat, while the earth began to make the low rumbling sounds of an upset stomach.

The Flores brothers, taking backward steps, almost stumbling on knotty roots, the twisted thick body of a sea serpent on land, an invisible fat vine the circumference of a grown man's arm creeping along the ground, José Matías and Wilber Eduardo, making for the safety of another tree, looking out from behind a gumbo-limbo, this time for sure, the *chaká*, known as the *sip' che'*, shielding their eyes from a glow whose source was the *tihuilote* tree, a trembling tree, almost shining with a soft tremulous light, its rotating tricorne bearing three faces, and the Flores brothers, taking a breath of happiness, mingled with the stuffy threat of an unforeseen disaster, yet lightheaded, and a lungful of air, the air increasingly thin, rarefied, low in density as the *tihuilote* tree, requiring more oxygen, sucking the air out of their mouths as they were trying to take it in, José Matías and Wilber Eduardo, their lungs complaining of the seemingly high altitude, as far as they could tell, two pairs of lungs feeling the pinch, and the magic dogs, beyond danger, they didn't breathe the same air as man, nothing to worry about, the *cadejos,* acknowledging that the Flores brothers were handling themselves well, they didn't have to lift a paw to help them, paws resembling the hooves of a deer, there to protect the Flores brothers in the likelihood of unpredictable events, faithful *cadejos,* in the presence of the monster that'd become a *tihuilote* tree, according to laws of nature, a reversal, as specified by Blanca's talisman, a transformation in the scheme of things, part of José Matías' and Wilber Eduardo's journey, and José Matías, it's been a hell of a ride, *mi hermano,* but as the word journey went through their minds, a greater distance than going for a ride, the Flores brothers felt a slight shock — it was the weight and meaning of what they were witnessing while hiding behind the *sip' che'* — and for a brief second, it seemed as if a dark hand laid hold of their hearts, with a warning from the magic dogs, *¡cuidado! ¡cuidado!* and a watch-your-step! the Flores brothers asking themselves questions, wanting to abandon their post, the *cadejos,* there's room for uncertainty and doubt, you're climbing through a chink that's barely a chink, but it's no time to be faint-hearted, and the Flores brothers knowing firsthand — now you see it! — the transmutation of physical reality into a higher spiritual realm, the *tihuilote* tree making the ground rise, fall and roll with the power of an earthquake, José Matías and Wilber Eduardo losing their footing for an instant, with a measure of doubt, but eager to follow the blind instruments of a benevolent Providence, whatever they were, and José Matías, I don't have the slightest idea what's going on here, Wilber Eduardo, it's more than I can understand, but a voice is telling me we've got to wait for a shimmering green light, exotic and obscene, maybe a brilliant flame like a ghost-light, and José Matías, the darkness is getting deeper, coagulating into a mass of inconceivable blackness, we're suckling uncharted territory, *mi hermano,* with this glowing wavering menacing tree in our line of sight! the *cadejos,* words of reassurance, don't worry! don't worry! just stay where you are, don't cry, don't run, despite the ploys and hidden dangers of the Evil One, you're saved as long as you stay put, and Wilber Eduardo, kneading his face with his hands, did you hear it? a bit too religious-sounding to me, and José Matías, what've we got to lose? José Matías and Wilber Eduardo, a kind of faith regained, won back by degrees without knowing it was inspired by the presence of the *cadejos* — ask yourself a question, have plenty of doubts, and when you know you haven't got the answer, rely on faith in God, it's a piece of cake, a picnic, kid's stuff — José Matías and Wilber Eduardo, not cowering, four clenched fists, a fistful of faith in each hand, knowing it wasn't a walk in the park either, fissures appearing in the ground, the earth cracking, expanding and contracting, yawning, breaking up, rising, folding over in layers, and the first prophecy of their future came to them while standing behind the *sip' che'* with the scalding breath of the *tihuilote* rushing at them in steady waves, a sort of heat mirage in almost total darkness, their eyes fixed on the only source of light, but unable to read it, the prophecy, maybe nuclear fusion, a nuclear reaction, powering a "main sequence" *tihuilote* tree with three faces, two of them their own, the third, a face they couldn't recognize on account of there wasn't much left of it, as hints and promises of their destiny, unmistakable signs they couldn't decipher, highway signs of warnings and markings blurred by speed and night, hurried undiluted toward them, almost knocking them off their feet, while a voice, the *cadejos?* or the fecund force of magic in the world, far from fairy tales and superstition, saying, bravery moves us to celestial spheres where the Goddess Birthright lives, reminding them of Anastasio Aquino, proud as a king, *Rey de los Nonualcos.*

The explosion was limitless light, infinite brightness, maybe greenish, maybe not, fireworks, bursts of starry colored lights and broad sweeping energy shooting outward and upward in the sky, rattling their teeth which somehow remained in their mouths, their hair no longer slicked back with Vaseline and Brylcreem, but standing up straight, and for an instant, nothing like it used to be, José Matías and Wilber Eduardo, looking down, wondering if they were still wearing clothes, seeing wind-swept trousers, fluttering shirttails, socks around their ankles, the Flores brothers sufficiently clothed to see visitors, no embarrassment, José Matías reaching for his pack of Delta Reds, patting his shirt pocket, they were still there, the Flores brothers looking at their hands, palms down, seeing bluish veins eerily glowing beneath the skin, but José Matías and Wilber Eduardo, shocked by the power of the explosion, almost enjoying it, standing on their own two feet, no teeth knocked loose, no bruising, no peeling skin, José Matías, when, after all these years, I see the past wiped clean like a slate in school, if that's what's happened, well, it's hard to believe, a wide landscape's opened out around us like an amphitheater embroidered with ranges of volcanoes, and José Matías, don't count your chickens, *mi hermano,* we were never good at raising them, the Flores brothers, as if hypnotized by the strange experience — add it all up and what do you get — a whirlwind of thoughts rushing through their minds, the process of projection according to the rules of magic, having inhaled the smoke of the extinguished *tihuilote* tree, a smoke which let them step out of their bodies and cross the threshold of death, just to take a look, and then back to life, a wealth of excited passions revealed on their faces, younger than their years, rejuvenated, the surrounding landscape was whole, the explosion had changed a thing or two, the Flores brothers watched the smoke clear from before their eyes, which at this time of day resembled fog, revealing all sorts of trees, shrubbery and plants, an evening sky drooping lazily over the outstretched branches of deciduous trees and evergreens and a newly born ring of volcanoes, the *cadejos* waiting patiently to see if they were needed, but things didn't look more dangerous for the Flores brothers now than when they'd first arrived to attach the branch that was a talisman to the *tihuilote* tree with three faces, and in the dusky light, sunless, the magic dogs, their white bodies gradually becoming transparent, on their way out after a long day of watching over José Matías and Wilber Eduardo, and the *cadejos* — instead of paws, they had hooves like a deer — speaking to each other, you can't say it wasn't interesting, their bodies almost completely invisible, fading like the sunlight that had long gone, and the Flores brothers, hearing the last verse of "Long Gone Lonesome Blues" by Hank Williams, Sr.:

> *She told me on Sunday she was checking me out*
> *Along about Monday she was nowhere about*
> *And here it is Tuesday, ain't had no news*
> *I got them gone but not forgotten blues*
> *She's long gone, and now I'm lonesome blue.*

A beautiful, melancholy song, José Matías and Wilber Eduardo, holding their breath, lyrics lodged in their brains, they didn't know why, but more of the supernatural, it was the musical magic dogs saying goodbye, not a matter of mere chemistry, the Flores brothers unable to bring a word out but unable, either, to conceal their feelings, after some time staring at what was once a *tihuilote* tree with three faces, they couldn't take their eyes off where it'd been standing, José Matías and Wilber Eduardo, not so much seeing as feeling the presence of a pair of dapple-gray horses, neighing, raising their heads, lowering them, nodding like they were agreeing to something the Flores brothers were asking them with their eyes, what have we done or said to bring you here? was it this? José Matías and Wilber Eduardo pointing at the empty place where the *tihuilote* tree had stood, two brothers a lot younger now with memories of their lifetime intact, old curses and old blessings, wisdom born of torture, suffering and pain, José Matías and Wilber Eduardo, looking through a window onto a new world, and the invitation, unspoken, of a pair of dapple-gray horses, sprightly and gentle, the Flores brothers, a wild joy, a wild impatience, the last mists concealing their fate blown away in the night, the dapple-gray horses, it's one of our little quirks, you see, you've got to humor us, it's one of the mysteries of heredity traveling down the endless chain of our forebears, we know the moment to offer you transportation, a discovery is near, your unveiling, don't be afraid, come here come here, nodding their heads again, agreeing to nothing, but the dapple-grays encouraging the Flores brothers, neighing, right this way to the ride of your lives! Wilber Eduardo, the question is, do we walk toward the things we seek, or do they come to us, drawn by our desire? and José Matías, adding to his brother's words, desire, or whatever we want to call it, *mi hermano,* why not desire! the two dapple-gray horses, a whinny not a bray, the cause is neither here nor there, so join us, Our Flores Brothers, and the Flores brothers stepping out from behind the gumbo-limbo, the *chaká,* known as the *sip' che',* where neither knotty roots, the twisted thick body of a sea serpent, nor an invisible fat vine the circumference of a grown man's arm got in their way, the fissures, the ground folding over in layers, expanding and contracting, yawning and buckling, moved no more, they were still, and still they would remain, knots unknotted, and an even path now lay before them, José Matías and Wilber Eduardo, levelheaded, kicking up a little dirt with their goatskin boots, walked with dignity toward the dapple-gray horses.

The dapple-grays, nodding their heads, we're completely serious, *mis amigos,* you don't think we'd try to pull the wool over your eyes, and José Matías and Wilber Eduardo, not wearing sweaters, the Flores brothers, looking at each other, saying the same words at the same time, as long as we're ignorant of the secret, which in our earthly existence remains hidden, José Matías and Wilber Eduardo, each standing on the left side of a horse, just in front of the shoulders, facing the opposite direction the horses were facing, caressing the dapple-grays' foreheads, watching two pairs of soft ears, placing a left hand on the withers, holding the mane to pull themselves up by the strength of their arms, swinging the right leg and pushing off with the left, pulling down on the mane, throwing the right leg up over the horse's back without kicking it, the equestrian Flores brothers, mounting the horses, no saddles, no block, finding their balance, two brothers sitting on dapple-grays with a night sky smiling unselfishly down at them, José Matías and Wilber Eduardo, looking up, offering a charitable gaze in return, a sliver of moon and the stars blessing them, the Flores brothers, each astride a dapple-gray horse, José Matías Flores and Wilber Eduardo Flores, a prayer to the Angel of Those Without Wings, making the sign of the cross, the Flores brothers, given unimaginable magic powers, earning a kind of divine status, leaving behind them the stress of modern life, at least for now, don't count the hours, nothing lasts forever, and here we are, we're here, the Flores brothers, riding dapple-gray horses away from the gumbo-limbo, or it could've been a giant *amate* or a tall *jocote* tree, and the maquilishuat tree, the *Tabebuia rosea,* its purple flowers with yellow eyes fading to white, it was disappearing from view, and a retreating landscape of immaculate parcels of cultivated fields, low and high grass, dried and washed-out yellow or almost luscious green, a broad, full mango tree, it wasn't an *amate,* that's right, you can say that again, the mango lost to view, and the gumbo-limbo, the *chaká,* known as *sip' che'* in Mayan, whose nectar is the antidote to the poison of the *chechen,* the black poisonwood tree — wherever the *chaká* is found, the *chechen* is near — the *sip' che'* receding, the Flores brothers without a rearview mirror to look at, knowing so many things were gone, the past, and the smoldering nothing of the *tihuilote* tree with three faces, a body that was once almost solid, a cloud growing denser by the second, taking on a familiar shape, a vision making their slicked-back hair stand on end, then a gaseous cloud, a river at floodtide flowing in reverse, growing less dense by the second, blurry and quivering like a flame, the *tihuilote* tree with three faces was no longer there in front of them, a memory ebbing away, nothing more, *ellos dejaron atrás lo peor,* and the lonely and large world as they knew it lay far behind them, José Matías and Wilber Eduardo, ancients of the tribe, a Laughing Falcon, *Halcón Guaco,* flying overhead, slow with quick shallow wing beats interspersed with glides, a series of notes like a human laugh, laughing with them, a falcon's laughter following the ancients, the horses taking them on another journey, where they did not know, rest assured, *mis amigos,* you've learned to trust again, to rely on someone or something, you're more than halfway there, the horses looking at each other, nodding and neighing to themselves, we've gained their confidence, the fine night enveloped the four travelers in its cozy blanket, the Flores brothers and the two dapple-grays wrapped in adoring arms, horses breaking into a gallop over the surface of the green-black waves of night, self-possessed and snorting, crossing rolling hills, real or imaginary, and in the distance the narrow silver ribbon of a meandering river, José Matías and Wilber Eduardo, passing night-dark woods on either side of them, the dapple-gray horses' fore-arms and knees, gaskins and stifles hurrying them along, places to go and things to see — they'd broken the backs of devils, banished ghosts — horses' hooves rising up in flight off the meadows, heading for the river, José Matías and Wilber Eduardo, all around them horses carrying other souls with trust-worthy instincts seeking a far-off, unknown home, a geography streaked with shadows, the Flores broth-ers and the dapple-grays leaving the earth, soaring above the river — clearly there were truths behind this illusion — in an intimate embrace within the circle of mutability, a bolt of lightning striking without warning ahead of them, strik-ing what or where they couldn't say, a fateful bolt, the white flame of an oxy-gas torch, welding or cutting, sparks flick-ering like match heads through the darkness, tiny sparks thrown off from what the lightning bolt had struck singeing their trousers, printing with passion irregular dark flecks onto their goatskin boots, a voice that didn't come from one of the dapple-gray horses, listen to me this one time, and let this one time be for all times, everybody in such high spirits, and on a night like this, here is and we have here the ecu-menical receptacle for storing the soul, look inside, a riot of fingers couldn't clean this bundle of dirty clothes that life is, a confession unheard at nondenominational unhearings in order to avoid storms, lyrical, refined, that's just the way it is, but you, you've hit the jackpot, *mis amigos,* so *¡uno, dos, tres, cuatro!* enjoy the ride! Domingo Zamudio, Sam the Sham, I'll say it again, *¡se sacaron el gordo, hermanos! ¡denle nomás! ¡disfruten de todo!* a cloudless night sky filled with stars, faintly lit by the sliver of a moon, a pure flame, on a nocturnal journey, so blinding was the unexpected brightness of a natural electrical discharge of very short duration and high voltage that the Flores brothers nearly fell off their horses, then observing each other closely, seeing the change within themselves, and the smile of certainty that illuminated their features, they exhaled with great force, which didn't blow out a candle because there wasn't any candle, the fickleness of magic, José Matías and Wilber Eduardo, that's the way it goes, sailing above the river, it mystifies the mind, a difficult kick in the ass, but it's our lucky day, so ride on! the voice didn't say anything more, and they galloped through the night in silence, no wind to give them a shove, it was the force of the dapple-grays all the way.

The Flores brothers, José Matías and Wilber Eduardo, sitting at Graciela Menéndez's kitchen table, with Graciela, Concepción, whose eyes were shut, smoking a cigarillo, Lucía sitting next to Emiliano, holding his hand in hers, Emiliano digesting a late snack, Gustavo rocking and balancing himself on the back legs of his chair, ready with a hand to grasp the edge of the table if he started to fall, Benavides, scratching his head before reaching for a slice of fruit, freshly cut mango, Graciela serving them whatever she had in the kitchen, and Concepción, opening her eyes, a gaze as straight as an arrow, so it was like that, *mis amigos,* and José Matías, yes, Concha, it was like that, and Wilber Eduardo nodding his head, nothing to add, they'd said it all, Benavides chewing without making a sound, mango juice running down his chin, Concepción taking the cigarillo out of her mouth, knocking ash off it into the ashtray, looking at Emiliano, give me a sip from your glass, El Puño, she always called Emiliano the Fist, but Lucía, don't give it to her, Leo, letting go of his hand, she's got a cold, Lucía getting up from the table to get a fresh bottle of beer from the refrigerator, looking back at Graciela, you don't mind, do you? and Graciela, my house is yours, Lucía setting a cold bottle in front of Concepción, take it, Concha, it's as cold as ice, and Concepción, *gracias, mi hermana,* an open bottle of Regia Extra in her hand, swallowing a mouthful, Graciela handing Benavides a paper napkin, wipe your face, *pajarito perdido,* Benavides smiling, cupping the napkin beneath his chin, moving it upward, an awkward gesture, slowly from bottom to top, until he reached his nose, and Graciela, you're fine now, go on eating, and if you want more I'll slice some for you, Benavides, a few words, a sweet-tempered memory, Benavides, we used to take walks kicking cans, looking for meaning, Leo, you remember? and Emiliano, of course I do, and we can go out later for a walk, after the sun's gone down, Lucía giving a nod to Emiliano, and Benavides, we can count the night birds, Gustavo, drinking orange soda straight from the can, let's all take a walk, and Concepción, a drag from her cigarillo, exhaling a cloud of smoke, a good idea, count me in, Gustavo ducking, dodging a drifting cloud of bluish-gray smoke, looking at Concepción, why don't you ever offer me a cigarillo, Concha? I might as well smoke one for all the clouds floating over my head, Concepción, any time, my Gustavo, any time, and all of them laughing, Graciela Menéndez the loudest, and Gustavo, I guess I'm thirsty, but I'd rather drink a beer, downing the rest of the orange soda in the can, making a clean job of it, José Matías and Wilber Eduardo, holding a cigarette between their fingers, lighting up at the same time, everyone looking at Wilber Eduardo, Graciela, Emiliano, Lucía, Benavides, and Concepción, together, since when do you smoke? and José Matías, you can guess, can't you, and it's no surprise! Wilber Eduardo with a cigarette dangling from his lips, no laughing now, a silence thick as a melon.

ACKNOWLEDGEMENTS

I want to thank Fermín Herrera, professor of Chicana/o studies at California State University, Northridge, who teaches Náhuatl, also known as Aztec or Mexican, the most widely spoken indigenous language of North America, for his contributions to my book. I also want to thank Hugh Hazelton, Associate Professor of Spanish (retired) at Concordia University, Montreal, author and translator, for his participation and support. My special thanks to Salvador Torres Saso, poet, novelist, and friend for his inestimable help, guidance, and a reader's pair of sharp eyes.

ABOUT THE AUTHOR

ABOUT THE AUTHOR

Born in Milwaukee, Wisconsin in 1954, Mark Fishman has lived and worked in Paris since 1995. He attended the Bradford College of Art and Technology in Bradford, England, and studied filmmaking at the San Francisco Art Institute with George Kuchar. He has lived in San Francisco, New York, and Los Angeles. While living in San Francisco, he participated in the movements supporting the Sandinista National Liberation Front and the Farabundo Martí National Liberation Front. His short stories have appeared in a number of literary magazines such as the *Chicago Review*, the *Carolina Quarterly*, the *Black Warrior Review*, the *Mississippi Review, Frank* (Paris), *The Literary Review*. He was the English-language editor of *The Purple Journal* (Paris) and *Les Cahiers Purple* (Lisbon).